Rivers West

Louis L'Amour

CORGI BOOKS
A DIVISION OF TRANSWORLD PUBLISHERS LTD

RIVERS WEST
A CORGI BOOK 0 552 10025 0

First publication in Great Britain

PRINTING HISTORY
Corgi edition published 1975
Corgi edition reprinted 1979

Corgi Books are published by Transworld Publishers Ltd.,
Century House, 61–63 Uxbridge Road,
Ealing, London, W5 5SA.
Made and printed in Great Britain by
Hunt Barnard Printing Ltd., Aylesbury, Bucks.

CHAPTER 1

A ghost trail, a dark trail, a trail endlessly winding. A dark cavern under enormous trees, down which blew a cold wind that skimmed the pools with ice. A corduroy road made from logs laid side by side, logs slippery with mud and slush, with rotting vegetation from the swamp.

Here and there a log had sunk deep, leaving a cleft into which a suddenly plunged foot could mean a broken leg, and on either side the swamp . . . well, some said it was bottomless. Horses had sunk there, never to be seen again—and men, also.

My father's house lay several days behind me, back of a shoulder on the Quebec shore above the Gulf of St. Lawrence. For days I had been walking southward. An owl glided past with great, slow wings, and out in the swamp some unseen creature moved, seemed to pause, listen.

Was that a step behind me?

Astride a gap between logs, I paused, half turned to look.

Nothing. I must have been mistaken. Yet, I had heard *something*.

My shoulders ached from the burden of my tools. Straining my eyes in the darkness, I looked for a place to stop, any place in which to rest, if ever so briefly. And then I saw a wide stump from which a tree had been sawed, a full six feet in diameter. The tree cut from it lay in the swamp close by, half sunk.

With my left hand I swung my tools to the stump, keeping the rifle in my right, ready for use. This was a wild place. There were few travelers, and fewer still were honest men. Young I might be, but not trusting.

For the first time I was leaving my home, going south from Canada into the United States. Westward, it was said, they were building, and we are builders, we Talons.

There was a time when at least one of the family had been a pirate. He had been a privateer in the waters of the Indian Ocean, the Bay of Bengal, and the Red Sea, but mostly off the Coromandel and Malabar coasts of India. He'd done well, too, or so it was said. I'd seen none of the treasure he was said to have brought away.

What was *that?* I half rose from my seat on the stump, then settled back, holding my rifle in both hands.

It was cold, and growing colder.

Behind me, on the Gaspé, I had left only my father's cottage and the good will of at least some of my neighbors. My father was gone. My mother had died when I was yet a young boy, and I had no sweetheart.

Of course, there had been a girl. We had roamed the fields together as children, danced together, even talked of marriage. That was before a man far wealthier than I had come to see her father. To be wealthier than I was not difficult, for I had only the cottage inherited from my father, a few acres adjoining, a small fishing boat, and my trade. And she was ambitious.

The other man was a merchant with many acres, a three-masted schooner trading along the coast, and a store. He was a landed, a moneyed man, and, as I have said, she was ambitious.

She had come to our meeting place one last time. At once she was different. There was no fooling about on this day, for she was very serious. "Jean!" She pronounced it *zhan*, as was correct, but with an inflection that was her own. "My father wants me to marry Henry Barboure."

It took a moment for me to understand. Henry Barboure was nearly forty, twice as old as I, and a respected, successful man, although I'd heard it said he was very close-fisted and a hard man to deal with.

"You are not going to?" I protested.

"I must, unless . . . unless . . ."

"Unless what?"

"Jean, do you know where the treasure is? I mean all that gold the old man left? He was your great-grandfather, wasn't he? The pirate?"

"It was further back than that," I said. "And anyway, he left no gold. None that I know of."

She came closer to me. "I *know* it is a family secret. I know it's always been a secret, a mystery, but Jean . . . if we had all that gold . . . well, Father would never think of asking me to marry Henry. He always told me you'd know where it was, and you could get it, some of it, whenever you liked."

So that was it. The gold. Of course, I knew the stories. They had been legend in the Gaspé since the first old man's time. He had been one of the first to settle on what was then a lonely, almost uninhabited coast. He had built a strong stone castle—burned by the British during one of their raids on the coast many years after, and attacked many times before that.

The story was that he had hidden a great treasure, that he could dip into it whenever he wished, and that he had bought property, a good deal of it. It was true that he had sailed to Quebec City or Montreal whenever he desired—even down to Boston or New York to buy whatever he wished. But I knew nothing of any treasure, nothing at all. If he had left any behind it was so well hidden that no one knew where it could be.

My father had shrugged off the stories. "Nonsense!" he would say. "Think nothing of treasure or stories of treasure. You will have in this world just what you earn . . . and save. Remember that. Do not waste

3

your life in a vain search for treasure that may not exist."

"There is no treasure," I said to her. "It is all a silly story."

"But he had money!" she protested. "He was fabulously rich!"

"And he spent it," I said. "If you want me it shall be as I am, a man with a good craft who can make a good living."

She was scornful. "A good living! Do you think that is all I want? Henry can give me everything! A beautiful home, travel, money to spend, beautiful clothes . . ."

"Take him then," I had told her. "Take him, and be damned!"

She left me then, and the next time we met on the street she walked by me as if I didn't exist.

My heart, I told myself, was broken. For a week I tried to convince myself of it. I tried to write poetry about it, I told myself my life was ruined, and I had a great time playing with the drama of it—but not for a minute was I really fooled. Actually, only my vanity had suffered, and that not very much. In fact, I was relieved. Now I was free to go out in the world.

Had not we Talons always done so? Those Talons, that is, of my blood. Others might have the same name, but we of our family knew from whence came the name. Our pirate ancestor had had his hand lopped off by a tyrant, had fashioned a claw to replace the hand, and had taken from that claw the name we bore. Talon.

A fierce old man in his later years, it was said. When I was a boy there was an old man in the village who claimed to have known him when *he* was a boy, and who never mentioned his name without a quick glance over the shoulder.

All that was long ago, and a mill does not turn upon water that is past, nor does a ship sail with the winds of yesterday. I had my own name to make. The story of that pirate Talon . . . well, that was his story.

A splash of water . . . a stir from the swamp.

The muzzle of my rifle shifted to cover the spot. It was an eerie place this, and I should be on my way.

Suddenly my throat choked with fear. From the dark, oily waters of the swamp, a white hand lifted . . . lifted . . . faint, ghostlike. It seemed to beckon.

I was on my feet, thumb on the hammer, ready to fire.

Then, slowly, the hand became an arm. It dropped over a log, and then a head lifted from the water. A strained white face . . . gasping, pleading, reaching out.

I sprang forward and caught at the hand.

It was cold . . . cold. But it was the hand of no ghost. It was flesh and bone. I hauled upon the arm, and a body emerged from the swamp and fell across the half-submerged log. Gently then, I turned him over.

"Help," the voice was faint, "help me, I . . ."

There was a stab wound in his chest, a deep wound from which blood and water bubbled. The man was dying. Even had I anything with which to treat him, his life still could not be saved.

"*He* killed me. He stabbed me. He knew who I was, he . . ." the voice faded.

"Easy, now!" I warned. I loosened his collar, then tried to ease his position. I'd no idea what he was talking about, nor what to do. He was badly hurt, but from the appearance of the wound and the bubbling, I feared the knife had penetrated a lung.

There was another stab wound in his side, and there might be others in his back. There was no dry land anywhere about that I could see. Nor any place to build a fire. To carry the man in his condition was unthinkable.

"Sir," I said, "there's not much I can do."

He turned his eyes on me and seemed conscious of me for the first time. "I know," he said, his voice suddenly quiet, "and I'd rather you . . . you didn't try. I'm . . . I'm sort of comfortable.

5

"Got me in the back. He's powerful . . . drove it right to the hilt three times before I got turned around. I don't believe I . . . I even scratched . . . him.

"A bad man . . . who'll stop at nothing . . . nothing at all." He caught my hand. "I'm Captain Rob . . . Robert Foulsham."

"American army?"

"British."

I should have known from his accent.

It was dark and gloomy. I was far from where I wished to be—which was an inn or stopping place somewhere in the five to ten miles that lay before me. It was already late.

He muttered, talked lucidly, then wandered. I stayed close beside him, irritated that there was nothing I could do, vowing not to be in such a situation again. Yet he was far gone and growing weaker.

"Get him!" he spoke suddenly, loudly. "He is vicious. A renegade . . . a traitor. He will destroy . . . destroy. He is evil. He is . . ." His voice wandered off, and he was silent.

"Who killed you?" I asked Then, realizing how my words must sound, I said, "Who attacked you?"

"Torville . . . Baron Richard Torville. A desperate man."

"What's he like? Is he tall? Is he—?"

It was no use, for the man had died.

I got slowly to my feet and stood looking down at him. What could I do? What should I do? I had no means to sink him in the swamp, and there was no way to bury him. Yet to leave him where he lay seemed a shameful thing.

If he had relatives, they . . .

Relatives! I knelt beside the man's body and went carefully through his pockets. There were some water-soaked papers, yet there were others in a sort of water-proof packet. In his pockets I also found several gold pieces, and in a belt about his waist, several more.

There was a pistol, useless until dried out and recharged. A small pistol it was, admirably made.

These few things I gathered together. When I reached a city I would mail them, for among the things there must be an address.

He was young, older than me but less than thirty, and well made. Somehow from his bearing I decided that "Captain" might not have been his only title. He had manner and style.

I had straightened from my final task when I heard a faint splash, a stir of something, a movement. My rifle came waist high, held easily in my hands.

Sounds came nearer, a step and a swish, a hit and a miss.

Who else could be on this road on such a night? Certainly, I had been a fool to attempt to reach my destination before night fell, and the captain here had been, apparently, pursuing someone. Suddenly a figure loomed in the darkness.

"Come along," I said. "If you're friendly, come easy with your hands in sight. If you want to be friendly, we can talk. And if you're not friendly, I can split you right up the middle."

"Avast there! Avast, lad. I'm coming in peaceful, wishing no harm to any man or beast . . . least of all, to me."

He was six or seven inches taller than my five feet and ten inches, with shoulders like a yardarm, and he had a peg-leg. He also had a black beard and wore a gold ring in one ear.

Armed, too. I could see he carried both a rfle and a dirk.

"You travel late," I said.

He glanced down at the body. "Did you kill him?" His eyes gleamed at me.

"I did not. Did you?" For certainly he looked the murderer, if ever a man did.

"Not I." He peered at the body. "Well, well. A fine, handsome young chap to die so easily. Oh, I've killed a few in my time, but not that one." He grinned at

7

me. "Anyway, I've just come up. You stand over the body, and the man is freshly dead. The law will ask questions, so you'd better think of some answers."

"There is no law here," I said. "This is the forest. Yet it is no way for a man to die."

The big man shrugged. "Who is to say where a man should die? He dies when his time comes, no matter where. And," he added, "only the body of the man is here. What was inside him is gone. Where he lies does not matter."

He gestured down the way. "I am told there's an inn nearby. Are you for it?"

"I am."

We started on then, leaving the body where it lay for lack of a better thing to do.

The big man wore an old cocked hat and a cloak that made him look even larger in the darkness than he was. "How far is it, do you suppose?" he asked. "I have come far, and this leg of mine, it does not favor long walks."

"Five miles . . . perhaps less. Sometimes the understanding of miles is not well grasped. Five miles can mean over the hill and around the bend, or it can mean all day."

"I know." He peered at me. "You've a load there. Is it tools you carry?"

"Tools of my trade. I am a shipwright."

"In the forest?" He stared at me. "You are to build ships in the forest?"

What my destination was, and why, was none of his business, so I simply said, "South of here are many seaports where they build vessels to trade with the Indies, or ships for whaling."

"You've a French sound to your voice."

"I am French . . . in part, but Canadian born, and pleased to be."

We walked on in silence, slipping and splashing, swearing a little and grunting. "I am called Jambe-de-Bois," he said suddenly, "because of this," he indicated the leg.

8

"It is as good as another," I said. "A name is what a man makes of it."

"True, lad. True." He glanced at me. "And you? You have a name?"

Suddenly, I was wary. Who was this man from out of the night, coming upon me standing over a dead man. Why this sudden interest in my name? For his tone seemed to have sharpened just a little at the question. Moreover, there was about him something vaguely familiar.

"Who does not have a name? I find them of small meaning."

Five feet ten inches, I was, and shorter than him. He looked to be a powerful man, but I yielded him nothing on that score. For I was big boned and muscled. In part it was inheritance, for mine had been a strong family; and in part it was my trade and the handling of heavy timbers. I believed myself the equal of any man when it came to sheer strength.

Who was he? And where was he going? I longed to ask, but had scarcely the right, having refused to tell my name. The vague familiarity about him worried me. I was far from home, yet this man had a feel of the sea about him and something of our own accent in his speech. Had he followed me? Was that absurd story of treasure to haunt me forever?

By fishing boat I had come from the Gaspé up the river to Quebec, had crossed the river and entered the forest.

We slopped along in the darkness, wary of our footsteps, only occasionally glimpsing a star overhead through the lacework of branches. Despite the peg-leg, he swung along as easily as me, and I fancy myself a man who can walk.

Suddenly, through the dark columns of the huge old trees, we saw a light. With the chance of good food and drink before us, we lengthened our strides and in a few minutes faced a clearing under giant trees and a ramshackle bridge over an arm of the swamp.

At the door the latchstring was out. We lifted it and stepped inside.

A fine fire blazed upon the hearth of a huge fireplace at the opposite end of the room. There were some benches, a long table, and a half-dozen men standing about. At the fire, a middle-aged woman stirred something in a pot that set my stomach to high expectation.

A mostly baldheaded man with a fringe of sandy hair, whom I took to be the owner, looked around at us. He wore a long buckskin waistcoat and heavy boots.

"Welcome, lads! Welcome! Come up to the table! It's a raw night for the out of doors. Have a nip of something. I've rum . . . even a bit of ale that I've brewed myself. Tasty, mighty tasty."

He turned to the woman at the fire. "Bett, get some food on the table. These will be hungry men."

There was a tall man with his back to the wall, a handsome man indeed, with a pipe in one hand and a glass in the other. He looked at me with a quick, appraising glance, then his eyes rested thoughtfully on me. My coat was open, and he could see the pistol there.

I set my tools in the corner, and after a moment of hestitation, my rifle beside them.

CHAPTER 2

"My name is Watson," the baldheaded man said. "We do a bit of farming here, and some'at o' fishing, and a man with a rifle can find game. We set a good table, if I do say so m'self."

He glanced from Jambe to me. "A tot of rum? Warms a body who's been out in the cold night."

"Aye," I agreed, "it has been a long way of forest and swamp."

"Here it is! And good Jamaica, too! I've a taste for the dark rum. Nothing fancy, just good rum."

The rum did take the chill from my bones, but it was food I wanted, and besides, I'd no taste for drinking with strangers about, and there was an air in this place I did not like. Watson was all right, no doubt, but I'm by nature a cautious man, and the look of the others was not to my taste.

There was a dark, sallow man with snaky black eyes. He stared at me. "Goin' far?" he asked.

"As far as a job," I said. "Word has come to me that they are building ships down Boston way."

Yet I was lying, for my interest lay westward rather than south. To the frontier town of Pittsburgh. Two or three years before, they'd built the steamer *New Orleans*, said to be the first on western waters, but I had a feeling it was to be the first of many. With the fur trade to the West growing, there would be a demand for fast, reliable transportation, and as the *New Orleans* had proved itself, they would build others. I had an idea of building my own boat to trade on the western waters.

The tall man with the pipe moved around the table and sat on the bench opposite me. His smile was pleasant, but the expression in his eyes was cool, calculating, and somehow taunting. I had a feeling that here was a man who looked with amused contempt on all about him.

"Colonel Rodney Macklem," he said, introducing himself. "Will you have a drink?"

"Obliged, but I have a drink."

"You didn't mention your name."

"John Daniel," I said it easily, but there was a flicker of irritation in his eyes, of impatience, too. Here was a man who did not wish to be thwarted or turned aside, yet his lips smiled in a friendly fashion.

I had just a thought, however, that he had expected another name . . . what name?

Jambe-de-Bois was watching me, too—somewhat puzzled, no doubt, and curious.

Bett Watson came around the table with one huge bowl of stew and two smaller ones, and with spoons and a ladle. "Start on that," she said cheerfully.

She was a blowsy, red-cheeked woman with black eyes. Untidy, but clean, and, I thought, a good woman with a cheerful air. "Theres more coming," she added.

Macklem lighted his pipe again. He avoided the eyes of Jambe-de-Bois, and Jambe did likewise. Did they know each other? Did they recall something each would prefer forgotten?

The talk in the room was rambling, mostly of trail conditions and weather, for it was these by which we lived. Macklem was casual, talking little. Of the body we had found I decided to say nothing, yet I listened for some word of travelers. One of these men might have seen his killer, one might even be his killer . . . although I doubted that.

The murdered man had been, I knew, a British army officer, and for some reason he had been pursuing the man who stabbed him.

Why?

Why the killing? This was no simple robbery, although every trail was beset with thieves and every inn a possible lurking place for them. It was no unusual thing to find a traveler murdered, or to have one simply disappear.

The cabin was more than just one room, but from the outside it had not appeared to be large. No doubt we would sleep on the floor in this room. Watson was even now stoking the fire, adding a couple of heavy logs that would hold the fire through the night.

The stew tasted good. When it was finished, Bett Watson brought us a big chunk of plum pudding and a pot of coffee.

Aside from Macklem, those in the room were a

rough-looking crew, yet I suspect I looked equally rough myself.

He said, "You are French?"

"In part."

"You have a familiar look, John Daniel. I think I have seen you before, or someone very much like you."

I shrugged. "Perhaps. Who knows? I have been here and there."

He was not satisfied, and continued to talk, but his comments were leading, his questions insidious. Obviously, he wished very much to know who I was, and he was not satisfied that I was a shipwright. Yet, he was pleasant enough, and an agreeable talker.

The air in the room was close and warm, too warm. I felt sleepy, tired from the hike. Not that I had walked far, for twenty miles was nothing exceptional, but the walking had been rough, the footing uncertain. Yet I did not want to sleep. Not until they all did.

Suddenly I thought of the waterproof envelope inside my shirt, and the water-soaked papers. There'd been no chance to look at them. The dead man must have somebody who would know about relatives, and if he was still in the army, his superiors would want to know of his death.

Watson and one of the others moved the table aside, and we spread our beds on the floor. All of us carried blankets—a man couldn't travel without them. And even in the larger taverns, a man was often expected to have his own bedding.

Long after the candles were blown out and only the firelight played on the ceiling, I lay awake, considering.

That man had been murdered for a reason. He was following the man who had fatally stabbed him when he had fallen or been thrown into the swamp. Therefore, the murderer could assume no body would be found, and that he was free from worry.

Two other considerations remained. Either the

murderer had searched the body, or he had not. If he had searched it, he had not wanted either the gold or the papers or the pistol. If he had not been able to search the body, he might still want those papers, if they were of value to him.

In any event, it behooved me to be very careful; to let no one know I'd seen the dead man or talked to him or examined the body.

Jambe knew, but had shown no urge to discuss it. Was he the murderer? Might he not have concealed himself when he heard me coming?

Under my blankets I drew out my knife. My work often called for a knife, and most men carried them as a tool if not as a weapon. Mine was razor-sharp, with a point like a needle. With the knife in my hand, I went to sleep.

The last thing I recalled was firelight flickering on the ceiling; then, shocked awake, I saw a dim red glow with a black figure looming above me and my blanket drawn back. A hand reached for the inside of my shirt. My knife thrust sharply upward.

Lying on my side with the knife in my right hand, I had to roll to my back to thrust. The thief, whoever he was, jerked away and vanished.

Vanished!

I sat up quickly, then came to my feet, knife in hand.

All was dark and still. Nothing moved. There was a faint glow from the fire, a reddish glow that flickered on some of the faces, threw others into deeper shadow.

Stepping across the sleeping men, I sheathed my blade and, taking the poker, stirred the fire, then added some smaller sticks. The fire blazed up, and the room grew lighter.

Six men lay on the floor; all seemed to be sleeping. I looked around the room. Nothing seemed amiss.

One of the six men was faking. At least one, and possibly more. One of those men would have robbed, perhaps murdered me.

Which one?

For a moment I looked at them, then I went back to my bed and lay down.

It was unlikely there'd be another attempt, but a man never knew. It might have been a simple attempt at robbery. I lay awake, staring up at the roof and listening. Light was breaking before I dozed off again —but only for a few minutes, and then they were all getting up.

After pulling on my boots, I stood up and started to shove the pistol behind my belt.

Macklem extended a hand. "That's an interesting weapon. May I see it?"

I tucked the pistol behind my belt and let my coat fall into place, concealing it. "You like to make jokes," I said, coolly, "I lend weapons to no man." And then I added, "It is just a pistol, like any other."

Over the table Watson told us the swamp lasted for only a few more miles, and the road would lead through forest.

Inside my shirt I could feel the oilskin packet, and my curiosity was a burning thing. Yet I must be alone when the packet was opened. The other papers had dried from the heat of my body, and they, too, might be revealing.

Jambe-de-Bois came to sit beside me at the table. "It would be a good thing," he suggested, "if we traveled together."

"Yes?"

"It would be safer, I think."

"For you or for me?"

"For both. I do not like the look of some of these," his gesture took in the others in the room, and he kept his voice low, "But I believe you already agree."

Why would he think me suspicious? Had he been awake during the night? Or was he, himself, the man who had loomed over me and then vanished so swiftly?

Yet, why not let him come along? If he was the man, he could be watched better when close at hand,

and if he was not, then his presence might be an added protection.

"If you are going my way," I said, "why not?"

Not until the others had gone did we gather our possessions to leave. When my pack was firmly settled and I had taken up my tools and rifle, I turned to Watson.

"Back up the trail four or five miles, there is a dead man. He was a British officer, and someone will be looking for him.

"Take this," I handed him a coin from the dead man's small store, "and see that the body is properly buried on dry land. His name was Captain Robert Foulsham, and it was yesterday he died. Put his name and date of death upon the marker."

Bett was staring at me, her eyes level and hard. Watson took the coin, then said, "How did he die?"

"He was murdered," I replied. "Stabbed. And he either fell or was thrown into the swamp. He lived long enough to get out and to tell me these things."

"Murdered? But who—?"

"I think one of those who slept the night. That's why I said nothing. Had I told you before there might well have been another killing."

"His possessions?"

"He had little. I shall write to his family and his superiors, and they will come to be sure he is buried well." I paused. "See to it."

We stepped off at a good pace, for I no longer worried about the peg-legged man keeping up; he was as good a walker as me. During my talk with Watson, he had said nothing.

Alone upon the trail he said, "You take risks, my friend. There are some things better left alone."

"Perhaps. But I am not one to let things lie. I shall inform those who should be informed, and then I shall go about my business."

"It may not be so easy. Once a thing like this begins, who knows when it will end? Or where?"

How dark was the swamp! How dank and dark!

We walked under the perpetual gloom of interlaced boughs that shut out all but scattered bits of daylight. The earth beneath was black, a mass of rotting vegetation. Old leaves lay upon stagnant pools, old logs thrust ugly heads tangled with a Medusa's weaving of twisted roots, old trees lay in mud around which the black water gathered.

The trail was barely passable, and every step was a risk of life and limb. Yet at last we reached firm ground, higher ground. The cold wind started up again, chilling us as it blew down the long dark trail.

Once we passed the ruin of a cabin, a worn fence close by, the bark falling from the poles, rank grass growing up to cover all that lay upon the ground and to make the cabin seem even more lost and lonely.

We walked the lonely road, and as we walked, we talked of many things—of ships and men and storms at sea, of wrecks and ship's timbers and the building of strong craft, and of the feel of a well-made ship in a heavy sea. I was no seafaring man, although I'd been out on the gulf many a time, had sailed to Newfoundland, to Nova Scotia, and to Labrador. When no more than ten, I had sailed alone to Bonaventure Island, which lay within sight of my home. But these were things many a lad from Gaspé had done, and although I was no deep-water sailor, I knew how to build a ship and what it took to make it seaworthy.

Jambe-de-Bois was more. He was a deep-sea sailorman, and no flying-fish sailor. He had sailed as bos'n, as sailmaker and as ship's carpenter. He spoke of Marseilles, La Rochelle, and Dieppe, of St. Malo, Bristol, and Genoa. He knew the Malabar Coast and the Irrawaddy. All of what he talked about I'd heard from childhood, for many a Talon had returned to the sea, and the old man of the family was not the only one who'd been a privateer.

Suddenly, I stopped. We had rounded a turn in what passed for a road, and there, a few hundred yards away, was Macklem. He and others.

Jambe-de-Bois swore, but it was too late, for he had seen us and stopped to wait.

"Be careful, lad," Jambe-de-Bois said. "Yon's an evil man, a sinful man, and one without morality or mercy. Give him the slightest chance, and he'll have your heart out and bleeding."

"You know him then?"

He was silent, as if he had said too much, and then he replied bitterly. "Aye, know him I do . . . or of him, and an ugly thing it was when first he crossed my bows.

"Watch him, lad, and trust him not for one minute. For some reason, you've attracted his interest, and those who interest him die. I've seen it happen."

Colonel Rodney Macklem waited for us on the trail, a bold and handsome man.

CHAPTER 3

"Quick, lad, before we come up to him—and speak low, for sound carries. Where are you bound?"

Hesitate I did. Who was he to ask me this? Could I trust him more than Macklem, who seemed the more complete gentleman?

When I hestitated, Jambe said, "We've more in common than you think, much more. He wants you dead, lad, and me also. Together we're no match for him, but we might last longer. What say you?"

"I'm going to Pittsburgh."

He scowled. "Pittsburgh? What is that? And where?"

We slowed our walk, and spoke softly.

"It's a new town in the West. There was a fort there

once, Fort Pitt. It's a place where rivers meet and where they build boats for use on the western waters."

"Western waters? The Pacific?"

"No . . . the rivers. There are great rivers there, rivers that go in all directions. Do you know the Mississippi?"

"Aye, I've shipped into New Orleans a time or two. Sure and it's the greatest river of them all!"

"It is not. There's a longer river, far longer, a river that flows into the Mississippi. It's called the Missouri. It's a river that stretches far to the west and begins in the Rockies. They'll be building boats in Pittsburgh to use on the western waters, and I'd have a hand in the building—and in good time, build my own."

"If it's water you want, why not go to sea? There's places out there, islands and harbors and such, that no man has seen, and many worth seeing again. Why sail a river?"

"Ah, but Jambe! This is a different river! The waters flow down from the high peaks, down through roaring canyons. It's a river nearly three thousand miles long, and who knows what lies at its head or along its banks? I shall build a steamboat, Jambe, a steamboat that will climb its farthest reaches. If you wish to come with me, I can use a partner, but I want no fair-weather friend. If you sign on with me, it's for the voyage."

Jambe was silent. Finally he swore, irritably. "Why not? I'll come along, John Daniel, if that is what you call yourself, for I've a thought we'll be safer together."

We came up to Macklem then, standing in the road with three others of the past night, the snake-eyed man among them.

"Come along," he said cheerfully, "there's safety in numbers, and I hear the Indians can still be dangerous at times, to say nothing of thieving white men."

So we went along together, Macklem and myself in the lead, and Jambe-de-Bois falling back to bring up the rear—but in such a position that if any attempt was made upon me he would be first to see a false move and not only warn but aid me. Yet there was a rankling doubt in me, for what did I know of him?

I was among enemies, yet there was a youthful foolishness and confidence in me that made me believe I could win out even if it came to blows with the lot of them.

I was stronger than they realized, and a better shot. Still, there was enough good sense in me—despite my vanity—to realize I might get no chance to shoot, nor even to use my strength.

Gradually, the trees thinned out, farms appeared. Toward evening we saw boys and girls driving cattle home from the pasture. People stopped to watch us go by, and some answered our friendly hails and some did not, yet all stared.

When we came to an inn, it was not like the hovel where we had stopped before. It was a spacious place, with two floors, glass windows, and a common room where drinks and food were served.

The proprietor here was a man of dignity, who spoke of politics in a manner that suggested he knew of what he spoke. But I was not sure. Perhaps he was no more than a fat windbag. There were aplenty of them about in that year of 1821.

Yet the linens were fresh, the floors swept, the food excellently prepared.

Alone in my room, with the doors locked and the hot water that had been brought for me in the tub, I bathed—the first time since leaving Quebec, and only the second since leaving my home in the Gaspé.

The open papers I'd taken from the pocket of Captain Foulsham were almost illegible. One was a letter, apparently from a brother. I could make out but little of it, as water had blurred the ink and made it run. The brother lived in London and was urging Captain Foulsham to return.

And I found his address.

Seated in my room, I wrote to the address of the brother in England. Carefully, I stated just what I had found, and how I had come upon the body of Captain Foulsham. I also related how I had gone through the pockets and retrieved what was there, and the money would be forwarded to him.

Moreover, I informed him I was quite sure the murderer was either one of the party that had come along from that time to this, or that the murderer at least was known to one or more of them.

Each I described with care, adding such fragments as might be useful, then I took it upon myself to open the oilskin packet.

In the packet was an order for the arrest of one Baron Richard Torville, a deserter from the British army, a traitor. There was also information to the effect that Torville had been an agent for certain forces in France against Bonaparte, but that he'd committed a murder and absconded with money that did not belong to him.

It was a long bill, listing a half-dozen crimes. A picture emerged of a man shrewd, unprincipled, and dangerous, but one with powerful connections. The title by which he was known was itself borrowed without right . . . there was even doubt about his name. The past of the man was shrouded in mystery.

There was no physical description.

Foulsham, an agent for His Majesty's government, had somehow tracked down and located this man—and Foulsham had been murdered.

Now I was myself in possession of information that could lead to my death.

Putting all the papers in the packet, I returned them to my shirt and went down to the common room.

It was empty.

In a small study opening off the common room, I found Simon Tate, the proprietor.

"Sir." I closed the door. "I have a matter of urgency and secrecy."

He picked up his glasses and stared at me, putting down his pen. That he was doubtful was obvious, but taking from my pocket the small stack of gold coins, I placed them on the table.

"I would like a draft for those, and a receipt."

He eyed the money and then me. Briefly, giving only the barest details, I told him of the body, that Captain Robert Foulsham was a man of importance, and that the money was to be returned to his family and the papers likewise.

That Tate was a man of affairs was obvious. His questions were few and to the point, and in a matter of minutes I was leaving the study with my receipt tucked away in my wallet and the packet left to go back to England by the next post.

Yet at the door Tate stopped me. Windbag he might seem when talking at large in the common room, but he was serious now. "This man of whom you speak," he said quietly, "is a dangerous man. Once a man engages in political intrigue, it can become a way of life. You must ask yourself now, as I am asking, why is he *here*, in America? Such a man does not only think of escape. You can be sure he has other ideas."

He paused, "Mr. Talon, I must speak of this to a friend of mine."

This I did not like. Yet I hesitated. "What sort of friend?"

"You might say that he has the ear of those who matter, Mr. Talon. He is a man who seems of no importance, yet when he speaks, those in power listen."

"Very well then."

"A moment, Mr. Talon. You have chosen to confide in me, and you have acted . . . you have acted correctly, I believe. So let us talk, just for a minute.

"I know too little of affairs in your country, Mr. Talon, but I would assume they are similar to ours. Let us simply say that here the people rule—but to rule is not enough. The people must also be watchful, they must care for their country and its future.

"There are many self-seekers amongst us, yet many

of those are sincere patriots. Our country is growing, but there are many forces, some abroad, some within, that are dangerous to us. You know of the purchase of the Louisiana Territory?"

"I have heard of it."

"Its borders are ill-defined. We have Spain for a neighbor on the south, and we have England on the north. I know that many of the English and most of the Canadians are our friends. But some are not.

"What we have most to fear, I believe, are those within our own borders who think less of country than of themselves, who are ambitious for money, for power, for land. Some of these men would subvert anything, anything at all, my dear sir, for their own profit. They would even twist the laws of their own country in their desire to acquire wealth or power. Such men are always prepared to listen to a smooth-talking man with a proposal.

"Are you going to stay among us, Mr. Talon?"

"I do not know," I said frankly. "I have come to this country because there seems to be opportunity. I am looking for honest work, success. Money, perhaps. I have heard they are building boats at Pittsburgh. I am a builder."

He nodded. "Good! Very good! We need builders, sir. We need them very much, but we need builders who build not only for themselves and for profit—and I certainly believe in profit—but for the future. Are you that kind of a builder, Mr. Talon?"

I hoped I was. Political matters of which this man spoke had never entered my life or my thinking. Nor had it ever seemed that the government of a people was any part of my consideration. Suddenly, uneasily, I began to realize that it might be . . . that it was.

"I hope so, Mr. Tate."

"Exactly. You must remember, my friend, that if we leave the governing to others, then others will govern, and possibly not as we would like. In a country such as this, none of us is free of responsibility."

"Yes, sir."

"What I am getting at, Mr. Talon, is that you have inadvertently come upon something that may be of great importance, and in which you are already involved. It might be very helpful if you would keep an eye on the situation . . . tactfully, of course."

"I don't see how I could do that. My immediate concern is to go west and find a job building boats for the western waters. I'm no politician."

He studied me for a moment, then shrugged. "So be it. However, young man, you find yourself involved. If what you have told me is true, the murderer of the young officer may be someone very close to you. He may suspect you have or had these papers. He may attempt murder to recover them.

"It has been said that the guilty flee when no man pursueth, Mr. Talon, but the guilty often suspect others of knowing more than they do. Your own life may be in jeopardy."

"I must risk that."

"And remember, sir, that whether or not you're a citizen of the United States, you cannot achieve success if there is turmoil or revolution or war. Good government is everybody's business."

I shrugged. "I know naught of government. I am just a builder."

He got to his feet. "I hope you continue to build, Mr. Talon. Good luck to you."

When I had closed the door behind me, I stood for a minute, pondering. There was much to what Tate had said. Good government *was* the responsibility of all. Even me, an alien and a stranger, if I was to make my home here.

Jambe-de-Bois was waiting outside the inn soaking up the morning sunlight. He squinted up at me, one lid half-lowered. "They left. Rode off down the road."

"They?"

"Macklem and them. He asked about you."

Macklem was gone, yet how far had he gone? It was not him so much as the snake-eyed man of

24

whom I thought. Were they a team? Or did they, like Jambe-de-Bois and myself, simply travel together?

My thoughts returned to my tools. Perhaps I should get a horse or a mule . . . or a horse *and* a mule.

The tools had grown very heavy, and the distance was far. Yet, if I could reach a river, I could put together my own boat and float down to Pittsburgh or its vicinity. I had only a general idea of where Pittsburgh was.

I considered my finances and decided we'd walk. Then I saw the girl.

CHAPTER 4

She was young, she was lovely, and she was riding a spirited chestnut gelding that she handled with superlative ease. Beside her rode two men.

One was middle aged and stalwart of build, a man with sandy hair now going gray, a broad face, a hard jaw line, and the look about him of a Scotsman.

The second man was young and good-looking, though not in the most robust way. Both men were armed; both rode good horses.

They came right up to the inn door, and the girl looked at me, right straight at me. "Young man, may I speak to the host, please?"

Something in her supercilious manner annoyed me. "You may if you like," I said quietly. "He's right inside."

Her face flushed ever so slightly—I was not sure whether from embarrassment or anger.

"Would you call him for me, please?"

25

"Of course." Put that way, how could I refuse?

Stepping inside the inn, I called out, "Mr. Tate? A lady to see you."

He came to the door, and his broad face immediately broke into a smile. "Miss Majoribanks! A pleasure! Would you step down, please? We'll have a bit of something put on for you."

He held up a hand for her, and she stepped down, lightly, gracefully, gathering her skirt as she moved to the door.

"Have you heard from your brother, Miss Majoribanks?"

She stopped. "No, Mr. Tate, I have not. That is why I am here."

She passed inside, and he followed. Her two companions dismounted, the older one throwing first me a quick glance that seemed to measure me completely and then the same for Jambe-de-Bois. On Jambe, his eyes lingered.

The younger companion got down also. "If you ask me," he said to the older man, "this is a fool's errand. If Charles were alive, he would have returned, and if he is not alive, what good can we do?"

"He is her brother," the older man replied stiffly. "She will do what she can, as her father would have done."

"I still say it is foolish."

"Perhaps, but she will do as she pleases, you know that. And if I were you I'd not try to dissuade her."

He shrugged. "I tried, for all the good it did me. She will not listen."

They tied their horses and hers to the hitching rail and went inside. I knew not what to do. I had never seen a girl who made me want to look again as this one had.

Their words I barely heard. I simply knew I had to look upon this girl once more.

Perhaps she lived not far away, for she was known to Simon Tate. Perhaps she stopped here often. It was a sparsely settled area, with many fields, meadows, and running streams.

On an impulse, I entered the common room and sat at a table near the window. Tate glanced at me, a little surprised. The lady and her friends sat with their backs to me. I ordered a glass of cider merely for an excuse to look at the girl again.

She was talking.

"Mr. Tate, the last we heard from Charles was from St. Louis. He was planning to go up the Missouri—that's a river out there—with a group of government men, scientists or surveyors or something. That was months ago."

"You must understand," Tate suggested, "that mails are slow, and the expedition may still be safe."

"I do understand. The letter was written many weeks before I got it." She looked directly at him. "Mr. Tate, I believe that letter was purposely delayed."

"Purposely?" He was obviously puzzled. "But why? Who would have reason to delay a letter from a young man to his sister?"

"Because that young man had suddenly come upon information someone did not wish him to have. I know my brother's seal. His ring is new. The seal had been broken and resealed. In other words, the letter had been read by someone else and forwarded to me only when they decided the contents were innocent enough."

"Please, Miss Majoribanks, aren't you imagining this? I mean, your brother is an ambitious student. He is a naturalist of particular skill . . . a known man in his field. But he has a way of becoming deeply involved in his work, of losing himself in it. I believe you should have patience."

"I know my brother is in serious trouble, Mr. Tate. He may have been murdered or held prisoner. I mean to go west and find out for myself."

"Please, please!" Tate protested. "This is all romance. You have no certain knowledge—"

"But I have! When my brother and I were very young we used to play all kinds of games—war games, capture games, often fighting plots against the Republic . . . you know how children are. We invented a country, *our* country. We called it—and I don't know where my brother got the name—we called it 'Iggisfeld.' "

"I understand, but—"

"You do *not* understand. Please listen. There was a girl next door whom we both detested. She learned of our game, eavesdropping, I suspect, and she teased us about it. Her name was Pucinara . . . I mean, it really was. So to us 'Pucinara' became a name, our name, for the enemy."

"Yes, of course, but I scarcely see—"

"Please, Mr. Tate, read this." She handed him a sheet of paper.

Simon Tate took the paper, and, fortunately for me, he read aloud.

After a brief account of his health, travels, and general condition, Charles Majoribanks listed a dozen or so plants by their common or botanical names and followed with several butterflies and spiders observed. Then he added, *"You will be interested to know that I have come upon a particularly dangerous infection, a form of the Pucinara, which, if left unchecked, will be a grave danger to the Iggisfeld. I must follow this up, and if not prevented, will forward my conclusions to you. You will know those scholars best able to deal with this material."*

Simon Tate paused when he had finished reading, then reread the message again to himself.

"So I've come to you, Mr. Tate. You are an innkeeper and a cattle dealer, but you are also a man with wide knowledge of affairs. What should we do about this."

Tate looked at the message again, then looked at her. "What do you believe it means?"

"Mr. Tate, the plants and other wild life listed were all known to my brother before he left home. There

28

would be no purpose in his sending me such a list except to lend obscurity to what follows, which is the real message.

"My brother has come upon some plot, some people he believes are dangerous to the country. This is his way of communicating that information to me. Obviously, he suspected his letter would be opened and read, and he wished it to sound harmless while yet telling us what he wished us to know."

Tate stared thoughtfully at the letter.

"Mr. Tate, the Louisiana Territory once belonged to France. It also belonged to Spain. There are those in both countries who might regret that it has fallen into our hands.

"There is unrest in Mexico, Mr. Tate, and I know enough of what is happening in New Orleans to know that every loose-footed adventurer in that part of the world is gathering there or in St. Louis or Pittsburgh or Lexington . . . expecting something to happen."

"You seem well informed."

She was intelligent, and she was assured. I was surprised to see how assured. Yet as she continued to talk, I could see why she had reason to be.

"Mr. Tate, you knew my father?"

"Of course. I respected him very much, a very astute businessman and trader. He made few mistakes."

"He made *no* mistakes. And he made none because he had information, the very best information and much more information than anyone else. He took care to see that his news was not only the latest but the best."

"How do you mean?"

"Mr. Tate, did you ever hear of the Fuggers?"

"Yes . . . I believe so. Weren't they a very old people, merchants of some sort?"

"They were. Merchants, moneylenders, men who financed trade and even financed Charles V, an emperor and one of the most powerful men of his time.

"The Fuggers began as simple weavers, Mr. Tate. They were peasants, weaving in their cottages. Then,

3

in the fourteenth century, one of them became a merchant. Within a few years they achieved great wealth, partly because one of them created fustian, a weaving of cotton and linen, but mostly because they gathered information.

• "They were a large family and soon scattered over Europe, but they exchanged their information. Their agents sent them information, their ship captains did likewise. It was the major reason for their wealth and power—they always knew a good deal more than those with whom they dealt.

"If there was a crop failure in Russia, they knew it. If a ship with valuable cargo sank off the coast of Greece, they were the first to hear of it. They knew what was in surplus and what was likely to be scarce, and they bought or sold accordingly."

"But what has this to do with us?"

"Simply that my father took a leaf from their book. He financed traders among the Indians; he had friends among the soldiers, among the flatboat men, among itinerant preachers. He received letters from all over the country, letters that told him who was going where and what was happening.

"There was no mystery about it. He wrote letters, he requested answers, he even paid for information. At the time of my father's death, he had over one hundred correspondents in this country and in Europe."

"I see."

"You *begin* to see, Mr. Tate. This correspondence grew too large for my father to handle, so my brother and I helped. We opened the letters, read them, listed the information in ledgers, and passed the most important letters on to my father.

"Since my father's death I've continued this correspondence. Despite the fact that we no longer live in New York and Boston, the letters have come, and I have maintained contact with all these sources and have helped to operate my father's business."

"I was not aware of that."

"We have excellent managers. They never knew the source of my father's information, nor have I told anyone but you, now. I have continued to advise them to buy and sell, and we have continued to profit."

I don't think she knew I was present.

"And you have information that something is wrong in the South, in the West?"

"Let me say I had grounds for suspicion. And then this letter from my brother. When I received it, I acted at once. I got out the ledgers and read all the information we had on the Louisiana Territory, read the reports of Lewis and Clark and the letters from James Mackay. My father had an agent in Santa Fe for many years, Mr. Tate, and I read his reports.

"Then I read letters from New Orleans, from Madrid, from Paris and La Rochelle. I made notes. Some items I recalled. Now I am sure. What my brother has discovered, Mr. Tate, is a plot to seize the Louisiana Territory and to make an independent kingdom of it."

"That's nonsense."

She shrugged. "Exactly the reaction from our senator, Mr. Tate. I approached him on the matter. He either does not believe anything I say or has reasons for not wishing to believe."

"Miss Majoribanks, you must remember, you are a very *young* lady. You are in fact—?"

"Nineteen, Mr. Tate, and for all those years I sat at my father's knee. For most of those years I had access to his office. I learned how to read from those letters of his."

"That may be, but—"

"Mr. Tate, I know you have connections of your own. I know some of your political affiliations. I have told you all this not only to give you my reasons for going west, but because I hope you will see the necessity for prompt action.

"The man who is to direct the subversive movements in the Louisiana Territory may already be en route. I know much of this man. He is a devil incarnate, who will stop at nothing."

Tate smiled, shrugging. "Your worry about our country does you credit, but it is highly unlikely that what you fear is true. They would need an army, supplies, munitions."

"They will have them."

"Miss Majoribanks, if half you suggest be true, it would be utter folly for you to go west. Your brother is a man of judgment. He will handle his own situation, and you can do nothing there but make it more difficult for him. Also, despite your information, I think your fears are exaggerated. No man would have the audacity or the skill to attempt such a thing."

"Baron Torville would."

CHAPTER 5

"Torville!" I almost dropped my glass, and I am a man not easily startled.

She turned to look at me, aware of my presence for the first time. "You have been eavesdropping on a conversation that is no concern of yours!" she said with anger.

"I beg your pardon," I replied sincerely. "I am drinking my cider. It was impossible not to overhear your conversation."

Simon Tate but glanced at me. Both the men who accompanied her looked over at me, the younger with obvious disapproval, the older with a careful measuring look.

The conversation continued, but in lower tones. I heard nothing more that made sense, yet I needed little more. Haughty the young lady might be, but she was obviously well informed, and I had great respect for her sources of information. My family knew about the Fuggers. The earliest Talon had dealings with them, may even have written some of those letters of which she spoke. In fact, he had himself used somewhat the same methods to keep abreast of changing situations in India, China, and the Malays.

In the days of his privateering, this Talon had been active in those waters, and in fact, his own wife had come from India.

If the girl's information was correct, Torville was the leader—or one of the leaders—of a plot to seize the Louisana Territory and set up an independent kingdom. It seemed a wild scheme, yet there were many reasons why it might be successful. Not until 1818 had a firm boundary been established between the United States and Canada along the forty-ninth parallel from the Rainy Lake to the Rockies.

Only recently had the treaty been signed with Spain ceding Florida to the United States and defining the western border of the Louisana Purchase at the forty-second parallel. The United States had renounced claims to Texas, and rights to many parts of this great new land were openly disputed.

But many Americans believed reports from various officers of the army that the great plains were a vast wasteland, the so-called Great American Desert, and therefore totally unfit for cultivation or settlement. The result was that few Americans believed the area worth fighting for.

In Mexico there was a growing movement for independence from Spain and the prospects of fighting had lured adventurers and soldiers-of-fortune from all over the world, most of whom had gathered in New Orleans to await the turn of events that might offer them opportunity for sudden wealth, looting, or whatever the chance offered.

Rumors of gold in the far western lands, mostly originating in Santa Fe and Mexico itself, had lured others.

Moreover, the changing status of the slave trade had caused a number of slave traders to abandon the sea. In 1808 a law had been passed forbidding the importation of slaves into the United States, and even now a bill was before Congress that would make foreign slave trade an act of piracy punishable by death. Although the smuggling of slaves would almost certainly continue, many of those traders who wished to take no chances were leaving the trade and looking for a fresh area for their talents. Much of this I knew from shore-side gossip in the Gaspé where the sailors from incoming ships were constantly arguing such questions in the grog shops along the waterfront. Jambe-de-Bois had, during our long walk down through Maine, talked of this.

Finishing my cider, I got up, paid what I owed, and went out. Miss Majoribanks' older companion followed me.

"Sir! My name is Macaire. I'd like a word with you."

I liked him. There was a broad, straightforward honesty in the man, and a sure strength that I always like to see.

"Mine is John Daniel," I said, continuing with the name I'd given myself before.

"You spoke of Torville. Or you seemed to know the name."

I explained, as briefly as possible, about the finding of the body and the papers and our journey since.

"You said nothing of the murder at the inn?"

"Not until the others had gone. There were some there I did not like the look of."

He kicked at the post of the hitching rail as he considered what I'd said. "They may still be around," he said.

"They may indeed. I do not know them, but one at least seems a bad one. A snake-eyed one . . . I'd not trust him. But I know none of them."

"Aye, I will speak to the miss of it."

"I'm afraid she took offense at me," I said.

He chuckled. "Likely! She's a proud one! But a fine, fine lass!" He looked at me. "You'll not be staying on here?"

"It's no place for a shipwright," I said. "I shall go where the building is."

"Aye," he agreed, "it is a fine thing to work with wood, and there's a deal of it here. The finest maple, oak, or beech. To build . . . aye, I like that. It is good to build. To stand up something that will last, something that will do a job for you."

He held out his hand. "Well, lad, here's luck to you. May the road lie easy wherever you walk."

"And the same to you," I said.

Jambe-de-Bois, who'd been patiently waiting, said, "Perhaps there's a horse to be had in the village yonder."

"We'll walk that way," I said.

Simon Tate came to the door as we started to move off. "You will go now?"

"Aye."

He walked over to me. His face was serious. "I will not be sending your papers. I will take them on myself. There is a smell to this I do not like."

We parted then, and Jambe and I walked toward the village. Walking opens the mind to thought, and so it often was with me. When serious problems beset me, I walked and let my mind ramble or, if need be, hold to the problem at hand.

Torville was not far from my thoughts, although I intended to get about my business. We had officials and all manner of men whose business it was to see to such as Torville, who was probably overrated in his villainy and likely nothing to worry about.

My thoughts came swinging away from the current

in which I wished them to go to muse about the girl, Miss Majoribanks.

Much as she did not care for me, I found myself admiring her direct, headon approach to things, although I thought her foolish to go into the West looking for a brother who might well be in no trouble at all. Mails were an uncertain thing, and many of those to whom letters were entrusted were themselves careless about delivery and apt to stop for a drink or two . . . or three or four.

The village was a neat cluster of buildings—a store, a blacksmith shop, a small inn, and a horse barn.

"We'll say nothing about wanting a horse or mule," I said. "We'll stop for a drink and talk of the way ahead."

A half-dozen men loitered outside the tavern. One was a large-bellied man with a somewhat soiled shirt, but a keen blue eye that took in me, my load of tools, my pack, and the wooden leg of Jambe-de-Bois.

He looked and smelled of horses, so I walked past him to the inn, then stopped and walked back. "Is it a place for a working man?" I asked him. "Are the prices asked not too strong?"

"Reasonable," he commented, "reasonable." He glanced at my load. "It takes a man of muscle to carry the load," he said.

"Aye," I agreed. "I bargained for a mule, but the cost was dear, and cheaper it be to carry the load m'self."

"It's a way of thinkin'," he agreed, but I could see that he was of no mind to carry any such loads and thought me a fool for doing so.

We entered the inn and seated ourselves near the window. Jambe went to the window that opened into the kitchen and asked for ale.

The proprietor brought it, and I paid him at once. He glanced at the coins in my hand. He nodded toward the road. "Tis a rough road for shank's mare," he said. "You should have a horse or two."

"Dear," I said, "a horse is too dear."

"You could sell it when we get where were going," Jambe suggested.

"Yes, I could that, but I have no horse and I doubt much if this village has a horse for sale, or a mule."

The large-bellied man then came into the inn and glanced our way. He sniffed business, and it had probably been some days since he had turned a deal that netted him profit.

The proprietor and the horse dealer were friends. No doubt one would often turn a bit of business to the other.

The horse dealer walked over to our table with a mug of cider in his fist. He pulled around a chair and straddled it so he could lean on the back. "Mind if I join you?" he asked.

I grinned at him. "You already have, but seeing you brought your own drink, you're welcome."

The dealer chuckled. "You'd not buy me a drink then?"

"When a man comes to sell me a horse, I think he should buy the drinks."

The dealer chuckled again. "Wise, ain't you? Well, young feller, I'm not saying I'd refuse a deal. And a fine, prosperous-looking lad like yourself . . . well, it's a bit rough for you to walk the country carrying such a load of tools."

"I'm strong."

"Aye," the dealer admitted, noting the depth of my chest and my broad, powerfully muscled shoulders. Muscles swelled my rough shirt. The bulges of my deltoids were like melons. "Aye," he repeated. "I can see that."

He continued to look me over.

"We've a couple of powerful lads about here. Too bad you're only passing. We might arrange us a bout of wrestling." The dealer suddenly narrowed his eyes: "You do wrestle?"

"Well—" I hesitated, long enough to seem doubtful, "I suppose I could. I am strong," I added, a bit uncertainly. No reason to let him know I'd thrown everybody who could wrestle in Quebec and Nova Scotia, and a few in Newfoundland. There's a good bit of friendly grappling done in seaport towns, and in going from one to the other, there'd been fairs and such. Often I'd wrestled, just testing my strength.

Of course, I'd had good training. I'd had the best, in fact, for it was a tradition in our family since the first Talon, that hard old man who founded the family and who had learned his grappling in India, China, and Japan. He'd only had one hand, but it was said he never lost.

He had trained his sons well, and in a hard, hard school. Even in his old age there was no softness in the man. And father and son since, they'd learned too.

Cornish-style wrestling, also, and something of the boxing they do in Britain. But there was no need to say aught of that.

"There's those about always ready for a bit of sport," the dealer commented, "and there's a local man . . . Neely Hall. He's a strong man, and wins most of the time. He's beaten everybody about here but Sam Purdy. Nobody wrestles Purdy."

"Is he so good then?" Jambe-de-Bois asked.

"*Good!* He'd make two of the lad here, and he's got the power to match his size. There was a wrestler came through here two months ago. He'd defeated everybody, and Purdy tossed him in a moment. He's a giant, Purdy is. Doesn't know his own strength."

Now such talk nettled me a little. I shifted uneasily in my seat. There was no man invincible, not even me, I supposed, and big men always got under my skin a little. That is, if they were the aggressive, bullying type. I didn't know that Purdy was, but such talk of invincibility stirred something in me.

"I'd wrestle him," I said mildly, "just for fun, you know."

The horse dealer laughed. "Fun? With Purdy? It

would be no fun, lad. He's rough. When you wrestle with Purdy, it's no fun. It's anything goes. You can gouge or bite if you're of a mind to, although the last man to try biting Purdy left here with no teeth in the front of his face.

"No, no. I wasn't thinking of Purdy. It was Neely Hall. I don't think you're up to him, but it might be a match. The boys would come out to see it, and there'd be some betting done."

He looked at me. "Do y' bet, lad? Or have y' scruples against it?"

"Well . . . if it isn't too much. After all, I don't know this man Hall, and I'm a stranger. There mightn't be fair play."

"Oh, there'll be fair play!" the dealer said. "They are honest boys about here. There's sporting blood, but its honest sporting blood."

Jambe-de-Bois looked at the dealer, a baleful gleam in his eyes.

"They'd be honest," he said coolly. "I'd be sure of that."

The dealer looked at Jambe uneasily. It was a quiet comment, but there were undercurrents of iron in it, and, looking at the one-legged man, the dealer felt a momentary icy shiver, as if somebody had stepped on his grave.

"Would you be for it?" the dealer turned to me. "I could talk to the boys. There's been nothing doing about here for weeks now."

"Well . . . I'm just passing through," I said. "I had not thought of it, nor stopping. It is a far way I have to go."

"Stay. Neely is about, and it could be done for the morrow. If you've a little money for betting—"

"Well. You were talking to me of a horse. I had not thought of one, but maybe . . . well, maybe I should use the money and a bit more I have to buy a horse or two."

It was Purdy I wanted, but it was plain to see

I'd have to go through Neely Hall to get at him. And I might just get a horse in the process.

"We'd best go," I said to Jambe-de-Bois. "I make no boast of being one to wrestle in a match. I have tussled with the boys . . . I don't think so."

"Come, now!" The dealer wanted his bit of sport, and after all, what was there to do in a settlement of forty people, with maybe fifty others within an hour's ride? "Nobody will get hurt. It is just a friendly match."

He got up quickly. "Enjoy your drinks, lads, and be having another on me. I'll talk to the boys."

When he was gone, Jambe-de-Bois studied me with some care. "You're surely knowing some of these country lads are strong? They wrestle a bit of an evening, and about the fairs. It'll be no easy thing to do . . . if you do. Have you wrestled at all?"

"Here and there. When I was a boy in school."

"A boy in school!" Jambe-de-Bois was contemptuous. "This will not be like that, and you'll be getting yourself hurt for no reason."

"I want a horse," I said quietly. "In fact, I want three of them . . . or mules. I want one for me, one for you, and another for the packs. So finish your drink then, and we'll be over the way to look at the horses."

"You're going to bet?"

"Aye. I'll bet."

He was silent, and as for myself, I was remembering that the breadth of my shoulders causes me to look shorter than I am. And the fact that every bit of me was solidly packed muscle over bone made me look fifteen pounds lighter than I was. This was in my favor—and then, too, they knew nothing of me.

But it was Sam Purdy I wanted.

CHAPTER 6

Fine horses there were in the lot, a couple of handsome geldings and a likely looking mare. There was a stallion, too, but a stallion along country lanes and villages can cause a man a deal of trouble.

But it was not these of which I was thinking. What took my eye was a couple of sturdy, hair-legged geldings, rough with their winter coats. Neither was over thirteen hands, but they were sturdy-looking, with strong, well-muscled shoulders and power in their haunches. And there was a sad-eyed, wise-looking mule, a black mule with whitish rings around his eyes. When he saw me studying him he tossed his head and yawned.

Jambe-de-Bois studied them with an unfriendly eye. "I'll have you know I'm no good a' setting the deck of one of them," he said grimly. "I'd rather walk."

"It is not so bad, and the mule yonder could carry our packs and the tools."

"I'll abide that. It's setting one of them takes me down."

We walked back to the inn and resumed our former table. The host crossed over to us. He looked at me, measuring my shoulders with a careful eye. "You're taking on a bit," he commented. "Neely is a likely lad, strong and a good wrestler."

"He's big, is he?"

"Bigger than you by thirty pounds. He's beaten them all but Purdy. Nobody can beat Purdy." The

41

innkeeper was quite serious. "He's more than a man, and he's cruel—a cruel, bitter man who fights to wound. There's those about who'd give a lot to see him whipped."

"It will come. If I beat Neely, I shall try him."

"You?" The innkeeper was scornful. "He would eat you alive."

It irritated me, this talk of the invincible Purdy. But the innkeeper crossed to the sideboard and came back with a piece of iron. It was a horseshoe that had been straightened. "What do you think of that? He did that here before us all. While we looked on, it was."

Taking it from him I looked at it, shaking my head. "You are right, of course, it took a man to bend that." Then I looked up. "The horse dealer promised us another drink. Could we have it now?"

When he was gone, I put the straightened horse-shoe down on the table, and when he returned, I said, "We'll eat now, for I want my food to settle before I grapple with Neely Hall."

"You will meet him, then?"

"I will."

"You'll be stayin' the night then?"

"We will, and mark us down for two good beds."

When we had eaten, we pushed back from the table, and when Jambe-de-Bois turned toward the door and nobody was looking, I took the iron horse-shoe and bent it double, almost back to its former shape. Glancing at it, I applied a bit more pressure, and when the innkeeper crossed to Jambe-de-Bois, I held it down by my side. "Your food is good," I said, "and the ale excellent. And just between us two, I think you're a likely man, but if you are also a wise one who likes to make a bit of money on the side, you'll say nothing of this to anyone."

He looked puzzled, wondering of what I was speaking. Then I handed him his horseshoe.

He started to speak, then abruptly he closed his

mouth and went to the sideboard. He thrust the shoe back into a drawer and out of sight.

The horse dealer came in. He crossed to the table and sat down. "Neely will meet you. Right here in front of the inn, at sundown today. Over there on the grass, yonder."

I shrugged. "I haven't said I'd meet him. What do I get out of this?"

"You can make a bet. You can make as many bets as you like, and your friend, too." He smiled, and I could see how pleased he was with the idea. "I thought you might like to bet."

"I've a little put by," I said with a shading of reluctance. "And, of course, you have your horses."

"Horses?" he was startled. "I've said nothing about horses! I thought maybe two dollars—"

I laughd at him. "You're wasting my time. I'd bet you twenty English pounds against the stocky gray with three white feet, the dun, and the mule."

His face shadowed a little, his eyes became worried. "I wasn't thinking about no such bet. I was thinking . . . well, just a sporting bet, a fun bet."

My contempt was obvious. "Sorry. You make a sporting bet, and I get my nose rubbed in the dirt. Fun for you . . . but what about me? Forget it."

"You won't wrestle?"

"Why should I wrestle for your fun? Sorry, my friend."

"But I sent for Neely! I told 'em all!"

"Your problem. My offer stands. Twenty English pounds against your three animals, take it or leave it."

He shook his head, but he sat still. Leaving him with Jambe, I got up and strolled outside. Standing under the overhang, I looked up the road. Some riders had appeared on the road, and I watched them warily.

They came closer, and I recognized Miss Majoribanks, Macaire, and Simon Tate. The younger man was there, too, lingering a little bit behind.

Tate reined in when he saw me. "You still here?" he stared at me suspiciously.

"Well," I said, "we got sort of involved. Seems they have a wrestler here, and they're trying to talk me into a bout. But this horse dealer—"

"You mean Kimball? What about him?"

"Seems like he's a tin horn. He wants me to wrestle, all right, but he doesn't want to bet enough to make it worthwhile getting dusty."

"Are you afraid?" It was the girl. She was giving me that cool, level look she had.

I shrugged. "Could be. But seeing as I've never seen the man, I doubt if I am. The one I really want is Purdy."

"*Purdy!*" Tate burst out. "You'd be wrong in the head to think of it. The last man he fought lost an eye."

"He might need a lesson," I suggested.

Miss Majoribanks just glared. "Well, of all the conceited—"

"Nice of you to notice, ma'am," I replied cheerfully. "But it seems they want me to fight Neely Hall first."

"You wouldn't have a chance. I know Neely Hall. He's very strong."

"Yes, ma'am. But when I offered to bet this Kimball twenty pounds against two horses and a mule, he backed down. I guess he doesn't think Neely's that strong anymore."

Kimball had come out of the stable. "That's not so! I'll take that bet!"

Miss Majoribanks looked down at me. "Do you have any more money, young man?"

"I have ten pounds."

"Then I will wager with you. Fifteen pounds to your ten that Neely beats you, two falls out of three!"

"Ma'am, are you sure you want to do that? I mean, I didn't think—"

"You didn't think a lady would bet? Well, many have, and this one will."

44

"Miss," Macaire said gently. "I wouldn't do that if I were you. You don't know this young man."

"I know him well enough to want to see Neely Hall put him in the dust!" She said abruptly. "Let's go inside."

Macaire offered her his hand and she stepped down, then went past me as if I didn't exist. As she passed I caught a whiff of some faint but very pleasant perfume.

Neely Hall came from his farm in a wagon. I first saw him when he stepped down in front of the inn. He was a big, hulking young man, a few years older than me, and much heavier. His face had a kind of boyish softness in it which mine had lost, and he seemed pleasant enough.

He scarcely looked at me when he came in, and there were no further preliminaries. We walked out to the grass and peeled off our coats.

He moved in swiftly, then suddenly ducked and dove at my knees with the idea of upending me, I guess. I sidestepped quickly, pushing the side of his head as I did so, which threw him off balance. He staggered, caught himself, and came at me again.

He was quick on his feet, although his movements were clumsy and untrained. But I wished to learn how much he knew. Several times we grappled; each time we broke free. The crowd had swelled to at least fifty people, and Neely was performing before his friends. I began to see from his approaches that he knew the rolling hiplock and he also knew how to apply a headlock or stranglehold, for several times he seemed to be trying for them.

He was strong and active, but I doubted if he'd had twenty serious matches in his life. Suddenly I moved in, but as I reached for him a stone rolled under my foot, throwing me off the least bit, and he dropped an arm around my head and applied pressure. As he did, he tried to work his grip back so his biceps would be at my ear, his forearms across my throat.

4

Thrusting an arm through his spread legs, I grabbed him by the buttock with one hand, dropping my left hand to his leg below the knee and bending it sharply back and clear of the ground. Then, with a great heave, I threw him over my shoulder and we both fell . . . only he lit on his head. Instantly, I spun around, dropped on him as he lay partly stunned, and pinned him to the ground.

"First fall to John Daniel!" Macaire shouted.

Holding him a moment longer to show there was no mistake, I got up.

Neely followed me, getting to his feet, staggering a little, and peering at me, surprised and shaken.

Of them all I think only three knew exactly what had happened—Macaire, Simon Tate, and the innkeeper.

"I never saw that done before," Tate commented, low voiced. "I thought he had you."

"So did he," I commented dryly.

We rested. I wiped off my face with a wet cloth and stood waiting. Neely was across the small circle of people, getting excited advice that was undoubtedly doing more to confuse him than otherwise.

Time was called. We circled warily. He was very strong and quick, and now he was more careful. I doubt if he realized what had happened any more than the others, but he didn't want it to happen again. He feinted a lunge, then lunged and caught me napping. He backheeled me suddenly, and I hit the ground hard on my shoulder blades, but kicked up my feet and turned a complete somersault, coming up fast.

Knowing how to fall is an art in itself, and the first training I had received as a child. How to fall, how to break one's fall, and how to rise quickly in a posture of defense.

When I'd gone down, he was sure he had me and came in fast. So when I turned my somersault and came up, I put my head right into a headlock. This time I was driving hard toward him, so I followed through and knocked him over backward. He took me down with him, and, as I broke free and started to get up, he threw himself against my legs and I fell again. In an instant he was atop me. In the moment he fell upon me, I had attempted to turn, and he had me pinned.

"Second fall to Neely!"

I heard the shout and lay still. I had started the move that would have thrown him clear but stopped. The time was too short, and I wanted no arguments. I wanted a decision win which could not be disputed.

We got up, and I went to my side of the ring. Macaire came over to me. I was scarcely breathing hard and simply waiting. I rinsed my mouth with water, spit it out, and mopped my face.

"You've wrestled some lad," he said.

"A bit."

"Yon lad is strong, but I saw you make the move with your feet. You were going to throw up your legs and catch him under the chin with your heels and flip him off, I think."

"I was."

"*Time!*"

This was the decisive one, and most of my money and whether we had horses or not depended upon it. I wasted no time, wanting no accidents. I moved in quickly, then suddenly ducked and hooked an arm around his right ankle with my right arm and threw my body weight against him. He went down, and I continued to roll with him, turning over atop him until I was in a perfect hold-down position, with both his shoulders to the ground.

It took them a moment to realize it was all over. The third fall had come so suddenly, they were unprepared for it.

Tate came over and thrust a hand under Neely to be sure his shoulders were down, but they were. My weight was across him, and I think for the first time he realized my strength, for when he tried to move I held him still upon the ground.

"Third fall to John Daniel!"

I held the position until there could be no doubt and then got up, offering a hand to Neely. He took it and got up.

"I'll buy you a cider," I said.

"Taken," he said, "and you're a strong man, a strong man, indeed."

We walked to the inn together, and the innkeeper refused my money. He leaned over the bar and whispered, when Neely was turned aside talking to a friend, "I made a bit on this, I made a good bit."

There was a light touch on my shoulder. I turned and Miss Majoribanks was there. "Your money," she said briefly. "I did not know you were a professional!"

"That I am not," I replied quietly. "I am what I seem, a man who works with wood. I wish to be no more."

"I scarcely think you need worry," she said ironically. "You have strength enough, I suppose, but to become something more needs intelligence!"

With that she turned away, her chin in the air. I was not angry, and she had a fine, proud way about her. I liked her lifted chin and the square set of her shoulders—even the way she gathered her skirt as she turned.

"And now for Sam Purdy!" The innkeeper said it. "But that will be a different thing, I'm afraid."

"There'll be no match with Purdy," someone said. It was a new voice, and we all turned.

A man stood in the inn door, a square-set man with gaiters and a gray coat. He was an oldish man, and a gentleman, by the look of him.

"No man will fight Purdy," he said.

"And why not, Reverend?" Tate asked.

"Because Sam Purdy was killed this day in Berwick, killed by the bare hands of a man to whom he spoke rudely and then tried to thrash.

"Oh, it was a fight! For almost three minutes, it was a fight, and then the stranger killed him, dropped him with a broken neck."

"That bull neck of Sam's?" somebody said. "Oh, come now!"

"He did it," the Reverend said emphatically. "Did it with his hands and apparently only half of his mind to it. You should have seen him move! Like a cat he was! When Sam went down, he simply took out his pipe and lighted it."

"Did this man have a name?" I asked.

"Aye," the Reverend turned to me. "He said his name was Macklem. Colonel Macklem."

CHAPTER 7

We rode as a party when we left the village the next day, and headed toward Berwick, a goodly distance down the road, if such it might be called. Miss Majoribanks and her party were in the lead, and Simon Tate rode with them. He would leave our group in Berwick and take the road down the coast to Boston town.

Jambe-de-Bois and I stayed in the rear, leaving Miss Majoribanks free of our company. She had paid off readily enough, and so had Kimball, the portly horse dealer, although he paid off with a sour expression and bad grace.

"Lucky for you that Purdy is dead," he told me. "He would have killed you."

"He might have. But he didn't kill Macklem, did he?"

Kimball knew nothing of Macklem, but Macklem was much on my mind. Jambe-de-Bois had warned me of him, but I had expected nothing like this. A man who could defeat and kill such a man as Purdy was someone to beware of. Well, our paths had parted. Nor had I regrets.

Tate dropped back as we neared Somersworth. "You will be going the same way as Miss Majoribanks," he suggested. "Macaire is a good man, but that other fellow . . . he doesn't measure up. Though he believes he does, and she believes him."

"It's none of my affair. I shall go to Pittsburgh. What they do is their own trouble."

"But you could keep an eye on them, could you not? She's very young, John Daniel, with much to learn, but she's also bold and fearless. She knows nothing of the world save from her reading. She rides daringly in it only because she has always been protected.

"If aught should happen to Macaire, I fear for her. She's like one of my own, John Daniel, and I've known her since childhood."

"She will have none of me. Anyway, I'm simply an artisan. I'm not a landed man—"

He glanced at me, sharply, I thought. "No? I have it on good authority that if you lived in France and had your just dues, you'd be at least a count . . . and a man of substance."

"Now who has been telling you that?" I was exasperated. "I am a simple workman. A man good with tools, and nothing more."

"Have it your own way. But you will be going where she is going . . . at least as far as Pittsburgh. If you can help her, please do so."

"All right," I agreed, not grudgingly.

He left us shortly after and took the coast road to Portsmouth and thence to Boston.

We, on the other hand, started south toward Haverhill, to then turn westward toward the Connecticut River. Our party was now five people. In Haverhill Miss Majoribanks expected to be joined by a companion, a lady whom she had previously known and with whom she had corresponded when she first began her plans to go west and search for her brother.

Jambe-de-Bois and I brought up the rear, riding some three horse lengths behind them and keeping our distance.

In Berwick there was much talk of the recent fight between Sam Purdy, who had been well known in the area, and the stranger, Macklem. Too late, the law had considered arresting Macklem, at least for an inquiry, but he had departed the town, and nobody saw fit to pursue either him or the issue. Everyone seemed more than pleased that Purdy was out of the way with no harm done to local people.

A hostler shook his head. "Lad, I never hope to see such a thing again. I never liked Purdy. He was a rough, violent man, given to brutality, and no one was ever at ease when he was about. But the way of it!

"Oh, believe me! It was the fault of Purdy! He was ugly and looking for trouble. I think he'd had a drink or two, and this stranger was too neat, too up-standing for his taste.

"Purdy started the trouble but . . . well, the manner of it. The stranger *destroyed* him. Literally, sir. Macklem destroyed him. You never saw anything like it. It was steady, deliberate, and efficient, almost without effort.

"No panting, no struggle, no cursing. He simply demolished Purdy. He must have struck him a dozen times, and a bone broken for each strike. Sometimes with fists, often with only the edge of the hand. But he wiped him out.

"Purdy was no coward. With a broken shoulder, the side of his face smashed in, he still tried. Then the man broke his neck. They can say what they wish . . . and most say it was accident. I say, sir—and I have seen many a fight—that it was deliberate. It was calculated, efficient, deliberate. Macklem knew he was going to break his neck, knew he was going to kill the man.

"And he did it, sir. Broke his neck and killed him, and Macklem with not a hair mussed. He simply tucked his shirt in a bit when it was over and made some comment about self-defense. Within minutes he was gone from the town."

Jambe-de-Bois listened, scowling a little. When we were away from the hostler, he said, "I told you, lad, the man is evil incarnate. We must avoid him. He will be the death of us, I tell you, and you ... you're too confident."

I was nettled. I did not like being disposed of so lightly. At the same time, the hostler's words were shocking. It is one thing to fight, even to kill. It is another when one does it deliberately, and without hesitation or remorse.

When the next day came, we passed over country which had only lately been settled. Although now the farmhouses were clustered more thickly together, there were still areas of dense evergreen forest as well as great boulders and rocks. The river was crossed by a remarkable bridge of which I had heard, as had many who work with heavy timber.

The Piscataqua Bridge was a really splendid structure, at least 2600 feet long, with 26 piers set in the water and on the banks. The bridge was laid out in three sections, two of them horizontal and one arched. The arch itself was said to contain seventy tons of timber. I could easily believe it, and took the time to stop, go under the bridge, and examine the work. It was beautifully fitted and assembled.

We stayed the night in Exeter, and not a word passed between myself and Miss Majoribanks, although Macaire was pleasant, and I finally had a word or two with the younger man.

He was really quite a handsome fellow, although he had a way about him I did not trust. His name was Edwin Hale.

"I understood you were going to Boston?" he suggested.

"It was a thought we had, but I am a builder, and the western waters are the place for me."

"The western waters? Or is it Miss Majoribanks who is the attraction?"

"I have scarcely spoken to her."

He shrugged, looking at me with a sly, rather taunting smile. "You mean, she has scarcely spoken to you."

"If you prefer."

He seemed ready to provoke a quarrel so I walked away from him.

The inns we found were remarkably clean and well kept, the owners of them usually men of some importance in their communities. The food was, for the most part, excellent.

At daybreak each morning we were off and riding. As before, Miss Majoribanks took the lead, and Jambe-de-Bois and I dropped farther behind. None of the roads were good. Most were only a few years old and heavily rutted from rains. But we kept to the grass along the shoulder and made good time.

The horses I'd won in my bet with Kimball were good, stalwart animals, not showy, but they were stayers. At the end of the day, they seemed to have as much stamina as at the beginning.

We stopped to eat at high noon in the village of Kingston, eighteen miles upon our way. It was a small place of some scattered houses, a church, and several stores.

Macaire dropped back with us. We rode for several minutes, and then he said suddenly, "John Daniel, are you carrying money?"

At my obvious surprise, he said, "It is not my business, but in Kingston I came to the street afore you and a man I saw. He was no one to like the looks of, and he turned away so quickly, I think he was not wishing to be seen. It's a notion of mine he's following us."

"No, I have little money," I said. I thought back to the snake-eyed man from the upper Maine woods, the one who'd been at the inn after I'd found the body of Foulsham. And I thought of Macklem. "But it is a good thing to know."

Somebody had stood over me that night in the cabin. Somebody had wanted to kill me . . . and perhaps they still did.

We rode quietly along, but now I kept a closer eye on the trail behind and the brush along the way. We talked of many things, for Macaire was a man who kept himself informed, and was keen in his judgments. And there was much to talk about. A man had just introduced the tin can into the United States, and was canning food. Some men named Daggett and Kensett were talking of canning fish in New York. And somebody wanted to introduce a bill that would permit Catholics to vote in Massachusetts. James Monroe was running for a second term.

The next inn was a pleasant place, surrounded by great old trees. We drew up in the shade, and several men were sitting on a bench in front of the place.

I had ridden on ahead. Miss Majoribanks drew up shortly. "Will you take my horse, please?" she asked.

I did so.

"Please rub him down most carefully. And walk him a little before you put him in the stable." It was an order.

"I do not work for you, Miss Majoribanks."

"What? Who do you work for? I thought you were someone Macaire hired."

She knew better than that, but I simply said, "I work for no one. When I work it is as an independent contractor. If you ask me to care for your horse as a favor, I should be pleased to do so."

"As a *favor*? Of course not!" She turned sharply away. "Do not do it then. Macaire will handle her for me."

Her shoulders were very straight, and I watched her go with pleasure at her beauty and irritation at her manner. She seemed determined to consider me a menial, and I refused the category. There was no work a menial might do that I would not willingly do myself . . . or had not done. It was her attitude that irritated me.

When we'd put our own horses away, I joined Macaire, who was caring for the others. "Have you seen him again?" I asked.

He shook his head. "No . . . but I like it not still. The country is alive with thieves and highwaymen."

"We are a strong party," I said. "It is not likely we'll be attacked."

Macaire considered my statement and agreed. "You carry yourself well, with your rifle always handy. As for the big man with you," he gave me a quick, thoughtful look, "he looks like a pirate."

"Jambe-de-Bois? I think he is a man to leave alone, Macaire."

"You do not know him?"

"We met on the road, and we travel the same way." I hesitated, but I trusted Macaire and liked him. "Sometimes I do believe he knows more about me than he should. I mean . . . well, perhaps when we met it was not altogether an accident."

Macaire gave me a thoughtful glance. "You are a shipwright, you say? Why, then? Why would any man be following a shipwright?"

I shrugged and said nothing. Macaire worked carefully, grooming Miss Majoribanks' horse. I liked the way he worked, swiftly, easily, with no wasted motions. It was a thing I valued, for it was so I had been taught.

"John Daniel," Macaire said. "It is a good name, but there is much going on here I do not understand."

I shrugged again. "It is simple enough, Macaire. By chance we have met. Your Miss Majoribanks goes to seek her brother, who believes he has discovered a plot against his country, in which a man named Torville is involved.

"On my way south, I find a man who has been stabbed and left for dead, attacked by that same Torville, or someone kin to him. He was or had been a British officer, perhaps a British agent. Now what was he doing on that lonely road from Canada?"

I had a new thought.

"Was he following someone? Or was he, perhaps, on his way to see Miss Majoribanks?"

Macaire straightened up, staring at me. His motion ceased. "Now why would the man be doing that?"

"Charles Majoribanks wrote to his sister. He may have sent information elsewhere as well. Foulsham may have been going to meet your sister . . . perhaps even with a message."

I was putting it all together as I spoke, and, of course, it was speculation, no more than that. Yet the coincidence would be great otherwise, and as much as coincidence interferes in all our lives, I did not like it.

Nor did Macaire. He went back to currying the horse, and I stood by, thinking as I watched him.

"One thing we know, Macaire," I suggested, "we are not alone on the road. One man has been killed, another attacked—"

He glanced up, and then I told him about the man who stood over me that night at the inn.

"We must be careful," he said, "very careful. I'd want no harm to come to the lady."

"Nor I," I said, and he looked at me, not too surprised, I think.

CHAPTER 8

Morning came with an uneasy sense of something impending, of something about to happen for which I was unprepared.

The common room of the inn was empty when I came down the steps from the room where I had slept.

It was a warm, friendly room with a large table, several chairs and a fireplace in which a small fire smoldered uneasily, as if unsure whether it intended to burn or not.

The floor looked washed and clean, and there were curtains at the windows. I went to a window and peered out. The inn yard was empty; it was hard-packed earth fringed by the green of new grass. There was nothing to allow for the feeling I carried, and when I straightened a voice said, "Looking for Indians?"

Startled, I turned, having heard no sound.

The man was lean, taller than me, and somewhat stooped. What his age was I could not say, although I guessed him along in his thirties. He might have been older. He wore buckskins, fringed, with a wide-brimmed hat, and moccasins on his feet. He, too, carried a rifle.

His gray eyes carried an amused look, but a friendly one. I grinned back at him. "You never can tell," I said. "An Indian might be any place."

He chuckled. "I reckon you'll do." He walked to the

fireplace and took up the blackened pot beside the coals. At a sideboard he got down two cups. "Been here before," he said. "Know my way around."

He filled the cups. "You the ones goin' west?"

Briefly, I hesitated. But I liked the man, liked his style and manner. "Yes," I said, "I'm going to Pittsburgh."

He showed his disappointment with a small frown. "No further? Pittsburgh ain't anywhere. She's a good enough place, but the frontier's moved west now. Pittsburgh and Lexington . . . they was the places. Now you got to go to St. Louis, on the Missouri."

"You know the Missouri?"

"I should smile. I been up it. Up the Platte, too."

His eyes took in the depth of my chest, the breadth of my shoulders. "You look fit for a mountain man."

"I'm a builder," I said, and then added, "I build boats. I want to build me a steamboat."

"Easier'n walkin'," he agreed. "Keelboat man, m'self. But mostly, I favor horses." He sipped the black brew and looked up at me. "You the one travels with that peg-legged man?"

"We're going the same way, it seems. We're also traveling with Miss Majoribanks and Macaire."

His cup had started toward his lips, but now it stopped, hesitated, then continued the move. Something in what I said had stopped that cup, made him hesitate. I waited, but he made no comment for several minutes. When I finished my coffee and threw the dregs into the coals, he said, "Mind if I trail along?"

"You're going on west?"

"I should smile. Back to the beaver mountains. I want to trap the cricks that flow down from the high-up hills. I want to ride the Crow country, the Blackfeet country."

He had been squatting on his heels, and now he got up. "He'p you with your stock." He put down his cup. "You say you had a woman with you? A Miss . . . ?"

"Majoribanks."

"Ah?"

I turned to look at him. "Do you know the name?"

He shrugged. "Now that's . . . an unusual kinda name, ain't it? English, maybe?"

"Maybe. She's American though. Old Yankee stock —and acts it."

He chuckled. "Heard she was right pert. Stiff-backed and proud. Well, that's the way a filly should be."

There might be two minds about that, I reflected, but we walked outside and to the stable.

He moved easily, carrying his rifle like an extension of himself, and when he went to work on the stock, he knew what he was about. We put down more feed for them, saddled up, and loaded our gear on the pack horse. He brought his own gear, and as our horse was carrying light, he added it to the pack. He had no horse himself.

"You'll not be able to keep up," I said.

He gave me a quick, hard glance. "You set your pace. I'll be along."

We led the horses out to the creek for water. It was a still, beautiful morning, and the creek ran cheerfully along, shadowed by overhanging trees. Morning sunlight sparkled on the water wherever it found its way through the leaves. The horses lifted their heads, water dripping from their muzzles. They seemed as pleased with the morning as we were.

We heard the hoofbeats as we turned from the water. There was a rider coming down the road at a comfortable pace. We led the horses back to the inn yard as the rider approached. It was a woman, and she rode a fine bay gelding—and rode it well.

She drew up as she entered the yard, her eyes going from me to my companion, then back to me. She was round-faced, pretty, probably on the sunny side of forty. "You must be that impudent young man," she said, staring at me, smiling a little.

"Well," I said, "I'm not sure I could claim—"

"I am sure! No man could be so broad-shouldered without attracting attention. Yes, you'll be the one."

She got down from the saddle without waiting for help, then turned to us.

"I'm Mrs. Abigail Higgs. I'll be traveling west with you."

"That's a fine horse," I commented, and she laughed.

She addressed my companion. "See? It has to be him. He meets a woman for the first time and comments on her horse. No wonder she thinks he's impudent." She turned on me. "Are you impudent, young man?"

"Don't plan to be," I said.

She laughed. "I'm for breaking my fast. Let's go in."

I tied her horse, glanced at the hunter, and shrugged. He chuckled. "There's quite a woman. Be careful, young'un."

Macaire was in the room when we went in, and Jambe-de-Bois was coming down the stairs. Macaire glanced at the hunter, and I turned to introduce them, realizing for the first time that I didn't know his name.

"Mr. Macaire, meet—?"

"Butlin," he said, "Calgary Butlin."

Macaire shook hands, measuring the man with shrewd, careful eyes. "Are you going west, man?"

"I am."

"He'll be traveling with us." I hesitated, realizing I had asked no one for approval, and so added, "With Jambe and me."

"He's welcome."

And then I said, "He's been up the Missouri and is going back."

Macaire turned square around and looked at him again. "I would be speakin' to you of that," he said shortly. "I have an interest westward."

"Aye . . . when you wish."

Butlin was an easy-moving man, light on his feet and graceful as a cat, which came from living in the woods and mountains. I'd done more than a bit of that myself. Jobs for a man with tools were often far apart, and I'd traveled by boat, canoe, and foot through much of eastern Canada, building boats, bridges, and barns.

I liked him. He was a wary, careful man who gave nothing in the way of advantage. When he sat down it was with his back to the wall, where he could watch doors and windows. From the way he did it, it was easily seen as a matter of habit, not a some-time thing.

Abigail Higgs who had been expected to join us in Haverhill, had gone upstairs to Miss Majoribanks' room. When they came down to join us at the table, Miss Majoribanks knew about Butlin. Nor did she waste time.

"Mr. Butlin," she held out a hand, "I am Miss Majoribanks. You come from the western lands?"

"It has been two months," he said. "My brother was sick, and I came to speak with him, but his body was buried before I could come to his side."

"I am sorry. Will you join our party?"

"I reckon I have, Miss. John Daniel here, he asked me."

She turned her eyes on me. "You presume too much! This is my party! I shall suggest who will join us!"

"Sorry," I said briefly, "I was not aware that I was of your party. We are traveling in the same way, toward an identical destination. I feel free to invite whom I wish."

She turned her shoulder to me. "You *will* join us?" she said to Butlin.

"I reckon I will, Miss," he replied gently. "But if there's to be a split, I joined him first."

Abruptly, she turned away and went to the table. Whatever she had planned to ask him remained un-asked, and I had an idea what the questions would be. Surely, in a country of so few white men, a man named Majoribanks would not have gone unnoticed.

We took to the road with the sun barely over the tops of the trees, but on this morning it was I who led the way—and with my own reasons. There had been a brief shower in the night, and I wanted to look at the road. My uneasiness was still upon me, and, though there seemed no reason for it, I am not a man easily disturbed, and felt a warning in the air.

Twice I drew up and studied the dust in the road. Calgary Butlin came up beside me. "Early travelers," he commented, and I thought there was a somewhat ironic note in his voice.

"Before daylight, wouldn't you say?" I asked.

He walked his horse on a bit, studying the tracks. "Rained about an hour after midnight," he said. "This was after the rain. Maybe two, three o'clock. You were first down. You hear anything?"

Had I? I thought about that. Maybe a sound was the reason for that uncomfortable feeling I had.

"I don't think so," I said. "It was a mite after four when I rolled out, and day was breaking. There was light but no sun when I came down."

He nodded. "Something woke me. Might have been horses." He looked at the dust. "Two riders. Unlikely they would camp out so close to the inn, and unlikely they'd ride all night."

"You think somebody was scouting us?"

"Could be. There's thieves aplenty in the woods."

We rode on for a few miles and then he suggested, "Can you get Macaire up here?"

I called him. "Macaire?"

When he reached us, Butlin explained about the tracks, and then he said, "I spent a summer hereabouts as a boy. There's a trail leads across country . . . old Indian trail to Albany."

Macaire thought a moment. "Is it closer that way?"

"Closer by miles."

"All right."

The tracks went on along at a good pace, but Butlin suddenly turned and dipped into the trees at a point where I'd not have guessed there'd be a trail. Then he pointed it out to us, a dim narrow track leading off through the forest.

Macaire took the lead, and Butlin dropped back

and rearranged the disturbed branches at our entry point. Then he brushed out our tracks and sifted leaves over them.

"They'll find it if they look," Butlin said, "but not unless they go back down the trail and track us to where we stepped off. We'll have us a good lead before they realize, I'm thinkin'."

It was a dim, shadowed place, and very still. We rode at a trot, then a walk, then a trot again. Twice we forded small streams.

By the time the sun was high, we were still within the forest, and we stopped briefly to spell the horses, gathering on the banks of a small pond. Nobody talked.

The stillness was marvelous. Only a few birds in the branches nearby.

At midafternoon we crossed a wide meadow and came down into a country lane. Briskly then, we rode.

We skirted a small village, and went back into the forest again. By sundown we had forty miles behind us, and we stopped at a large, comfortable-looking farm. The women slept in the house, the rest of us outside in the barn. I awakened to the smell of fresh hay and the cackling of a hen who had just laid an egg and was informing the world.

A quick check of the trail showed no signs of travel, and by an hour after sun-up we were dusting our tracks down the trail.

Albany was a small town that had once been Dutch. We came up to it along a very dusty road over a plain dotted with pines. The houses on the way to the town were few and poor. Albany had first been called Beverwyck, then changed to Fort Orange, and after that to Williamstadt and finally Albany. A few of the houses were still of the Dutch fashion, with high, sharp roofs, small windows, and low ceilings. Most of the streets were at right angles to the river, and there were some new, fine-looking houses. One that I noticed, at the head of Market Street, was said to be the home of a family named Van Rensselaer.

We ate one meal in the town, bought supplies, and rode out at once toward the west.

Now we followed no set route, but took bypaths and lanes or Indian trails, many long abandoned, across the country and generally down the course of the Allegheny River. Nor had we any nighttime visitors or travelers upon the trail before or behind, beyond occasional country folks, until we rode into the town of Pittsburgh at the meeting of the rivers.

CHAPTER 9

Macaire drew up at a corner of Grant Street. He turned in his saddle. "You are stopping now?"

"I am. I'll be searching out a job of boat building here."

"Luck be with you. 'Tis a far piece we've come together, and I'd wish it were all the way. You be good men and true," he said, "and I've slept easy these nights with the thought of you by."

Even Miss Majoribanks turned in her saddle, and I thought her features softened a little as she looked toward me. "I do not like saying goodbye," she said, "so I shall not."

"Nor I," I said quietly, "nor do I envy you the trail you go. Please be careful, for I think there are those who know why and where you go and who want no one so near to them as can see what they do."

"I shall manage," she replied.

They turned aside then, riding toward Penn Street where Miss Majoribanks had friends with whom to stay. As for Jambe-de-Bois, Butlin, and myself, we had no friends and no place to stay except what our money would buy.

Pittsburgh lay neatly between the Allegheny and the Monongahela rivers, which joined at this point to form the Ohio. Fort Pitt, originally founded here many years before, had been a point of much warfare between Indians and whites, between French and English, and the site was important.

We found a hotel close by the riverfront, and we stabled our horses nearby. It was the room for me, and a hot bath, but Jambe-de-Bois went along to the common room for a noggin of rum.

Calgary Butlin watched him go and then said to me, "I shall go along the street. There will be men from the mountains here."

We had not talked of what lay west, nor of Torville, so I said to him, "Say nothing, but if you hear a word of a man named Charles Majoribanks, I'd like to know."

He gave me a thoughtful look and then said, "I will come with you a bit. There are things that need be said."

In my room he sat in a window seat, cross-legged, as he preferred to sit. "He is related to the young lady?"

"Her brother," I said. "She is going west to find him. She believes he is in some kind of trouble."

"He is that," Butlin said wryly. "He's crossed the trail of some rather dangerous men."

"What do you know of all this?"

He looked at me directly. "There are no secrets in the West, although there are some who believe otherwise. No man moves but what someone sees, and no man speaks but what someone listens. Indians are curious folk, and often puzzled by the curious things done by white men. They discuss them over their pipes.

"There are men among the Indians who talk of war. There is talk of guns, of many rifles that will come from the sea. Men move from tribe to tribe

65

along with some disgruntled Indians, and it is said that many of the Indians listen with both ears."

"And Charles Majoribanks?" I said.

"I hear of him from time to time."

It was dark when I went out again to the street. There was a gleam of reflected light on the waters of the Monongahela, and I stood on the street for a few minutes, just looking at the river and listening.

From up the street came the tinny sound of a piano, and somebody whooped. Two men passed me, smelling of wine and tar, both a little unsteady. From somewhere close by I could smell the good smell of fresh lumber, and then I saw it, great tiers of planks stacked to season in the sun, and a cribbing of heavy timbers and poles for masts.

Yet my thought returned to Miss Majoribanks and her voyage to the West. Uneasily, I recalled my promise to Simon Tate . . . yet the promise had only been to see her safely here. Now she was going to St. Louis, and if she didn't find word of her brother there, she would go up the Missouri or the Platte.

No need to worry. Macaire was a good man, a solid man.

Yet worry I did. She was too young, too seemingly sure of herself.

I walked on along the waterfront, seeing several keelboats in the building process and at least one hull that appeared from its shallowness to be that of a steamboat being built for service on the Missouri.

There was a light in a shack near the farthest stacks of lumber. Beyond it, the bank sloped away, and I could see flatboats moored along the river. From some of them came voices, and the cabins showed lights in their windows. Men lived on these boats, floated downriver to New Orleans, sold the boats, and then paid their passage back upstream.

Suddenly I saw it. I stopped, caught in midstride, straining my eyes through the gathering darkness. The head of a giant sea monster or dragon, rearing up from the river and carrying a steamboat on its back.

I went down to the dock. The *Western Engineer!* This, then, was the boat that had gone west with the Major Stephen H. Long expedition. Even in Canada, which was far from here, news of the expedition had been heard. Thirty-five days from Pittsburgh to St. Louis, with several stops along the way. I looked at the name on the hull and the long, scaly-looking, serpentlike boat, her head reared up as high as the deck, her tail fins covering the view of the stern paddle wheel from the sides.

It was something to see, even in the dusk as I reached her. It had been built, t'was said, to frighten the Indians. I'd known a few Indians, and I doubted whether any of them would be frightened for long. Yet it must have been impressive, steaming along upstream against the current, smoke issuing from its nostrils, foaming water behind it.

"Like her?"

A man was leaning on the rail alongside her scaly back.

"She must have been a joy to build."

"Build? Aye . . . I'd no hand in that, but she takes the river nicely. I'd say it's a shame."

"Shame?"

"She's government built, and the government has had their fill of her. They're takin' her up the Ohio a ways, and she'll be junked."

I glanced at her hull. She'd be about seventy-five feet long. "How much does she draw?"

"Nineteen inches, fully loaded. She's right for the western rivers, where often enough you have to chase the water to find it."

"How about her boilers?"

"No trouble. She's a good craft . . . *good*. It's just that she was sent to do a job, and it was only half done. But that was the fault of the men aboard and the difficulties that arose."

We talked a bit longer, and I'm afraid my questions

were as much about conditions upriver as the possibilities of building a ship. The trouble was, I was beginning to feel the fever.

When a man came into Pittsburgh, Cincinnati, or Lexington then, he found himself meeting folks from all over who talked of only one thing: the West. Everybody had either been west or was going there. They talked of Indians, buffaloes, game, but more than anything else they just talked about the land, the prairies, and the mountains.

Sometimes it made no sense. Men with good jobs, professions, or businesses talking of going west. Many of them had only to stay where they were to get rich, but there was a drive in them that went beyond money, beyond success. It was the drive to explore, to develop new country, to populate those vast empty lands to the west.

It was in the air I breathed in that frontier town, and must be even more so out there in St. Louis, where everybody in Pittsburgh seemed determined to go. There was talk of opening trade with Santa Fe, talk of California, wherever that was.

This man had it, too. His name was John Massman, he had been to St. Louis twice before, and up the Missouri with a keelboat before that.

"Injuns? I've known a-plenty. Good folks, but notional. They can change their minds in a minute, and they think lightly of the white man. Most of them have seen few of us and we all want to trade.

"The Injun is convinced the white man can't get along without him. Buffalo robes are all important to an Injun, and he believes the white man has no buffalo to hunt so he has to come west to get robes from the Injun.

"A few Injuns have been east and seen the cities, but the other Injuns don't believe what they say. They call them liars, say the white man's medicine has confused them.

"You got to walk soft with Injuns until you know how the wind blows. . . . There's much fightin' amongst them, an' they raid each other's villages, catch huntin' parties, even squaws out gatherin' wood. . . . They kill them an' take their scalps.

"If'n you do business with one tribe, another's liable to make you for an enemy. You got to walk easy until you know where they stand."

It sounded like good advice, and I needed it.

Now the fever was on me.

I left Massman and walked a long time. It was very late when I went back to the hotel. Jambe-de-Bois was sitting in the common room combing his beard and muttering. He combed his beard when he worried, and he was worried now.

He had a glass of rum before him, and from his flushed cheeks, I knew it was not the first, although he was a man who drank little and could hold his liquor.

"They're here, lad," he said to me, "they've come up to us."

"Who?"

"Macklem and that lot. Only there's more of them now. And a rum lot they are, too! They've tied in with eight or ten rascals from God knows where, and they're fixing to go west."

"It's none of our affair," I said, shrugging. "The sooner they go, the better."

He shot me a hard glance, eyes bulging a bit as they were likely to do when he was overwrought. "None of our affair, you say? That may be one way of thinking, but I think we're lashed to them, sink or swim, until some one drowns!"

He took a short swallow of rum. "That one with the sneaky eyes . . . he was in here, askin' after you. He didn't see me," he indicated the rear. "I was back yonder by the door, and he asked partic'lar for you."

"All right, he knows where I am."

"And that wasn't all," Jambe-de-Bois wiped his beard with the back of his hand. "He asked after the young miss."

There was a sudden stillness in me. Jambe had all my attention, and he knew it.

"He asked for her?"

"He did. But nobody knew aught of her here, and he went away after a quick look around him. Oh, he's a suspicious lot, that one!"

Abruptly, I dropped into a chair across from him. Asking after Miss Majoribanks, were they? Now, why?

How much they inquired after me did not matter. I could take care of myself—or try. With her it was a different thing. She was a fine, proud young lady with no idea what she was getting into, nor could Macaire tell her. As for her other young friend . . .

She was going west to look for her brother, who had discovered, or thought he had, some kind of plot. Nor did I doubt there might be some such plan, for there had been many before. Some men were ravenous for land. The very existence of such a vast, unexplored area was a temptation to every adventurer or soldier-of-fortune, and each one dreamed of becoming king overnight. A king of his own vast land, vaguely reported to be as large as Europe.

The success of the Lewis and Clark expedition had only added fuel to their dreams, for if sixteen men or so could travel across a continent, couldn't a few hundred men seize it for themselves?

Swiftly, I reviewed the situation in my thoughts. A problem must be clearly defined before it can be solved.

She was going west. They were going west. Her brother, Charles Majoribanks, had somehow become involved in, or aware of, a plot whose seriousness I was not qualified to judge.

Only weeks ago I had come upon the body of a dying man who was somehow involved in that very plot, or one very similar to it.

The murderer could have been only a few minutes away at the time of my discovery.

The so-called Colonel Macklem had been stopping at the next inn, and with him a bunch of men who, if not rascals, at least looked the part.

Macklem had proved himself an exceptionally dangerous man by killing Sam Purdy.

Now that same Macklem was here in Pittsburgh, inquiring about, or having one of his henchmen inquire about, Miss Majoribanks.

It was true that I had warned her, but she had taken my warning very casually.

"It's none of my affair," I said at last. "She has been warned."

"Hah!" Jambe-de-Bois said explosively. "Warned! Did you ever know such a high-headed young filly to take to a warning?"

"Well, that's up to her."

"Is it? It was in my mind that you were having ideas about her. Not that I'd blame you, lad. She's right pretty, that one, right pretty!"

I growled something and tossed off my bit of rum. "I am for sleep," I said irritably, "let her go her way."

Getting to my feet, I added, "Anyway, she has Macaire."

"Macaire! Do you think he's a match for that lot? Macklem's a devil. A devil, I tell you. Macaire's a solid man, a good man, but he's not up to Macklem's boot tops. Macklem would swallow him whole and spit him out."

"I work with timber," I said stubbornly. "I came to build boats."

"Aye . . . so the girl can go to the devil."

"Who are you to talk so to me? You damned pirate!"

He laughed, baring his ugly teeth in the process. "Pirate, is it? *You* say that to me? Your own pirate blood runs thick in your veins. Do you think I bought that John Daniel story? You take me for a bloody fool! I'd know your like wherever seen, for you've the mark of the Talon upon you, and if you had a claw for a hand, you'd be the spittin' image of the old devil himself!"

Well! I stared at him. Who was this man who had

come out of the night and the swamp and who knew me by name?

We were almost alone in the room, and our voices had been low but intense. Several had turned their eyes upon us, seeking the beginning of a quarrel, or so they thought.

"If my name be Talon," I said, "so be it. Jean Daniel Talon, if you wish to know, and it is said the old man of my tribe was a pirate . . . or a privateer. What is that to you?"

He had half risen from his chair; now he sat down. "Sit, damn you, and we'll talk. You called me a pirate, and I have been that—and more. No better gunner ever sailed the seas than I, and sometimes I sailed under the black flag, but that be neither here nor there.

"Do you think those who sailed the Indian seas have forgotten the old Claw? They remember him. Believe me, they do, and how he took the fortress of Gingee, singlehanded."

"He did not take it. He merely entered it."

"'Entered it,' he says. Yes, he entered it, entered it when no army could have done it, scaled walls and towers right into the inner rooms and bearded the old lion in his den, took him by the beard and trimmed his ears, then killed him and carried off a bag of loot that would ransom half the kings of Europe! Who in those waters does not know the story?

"Aye, and I've looked upon the walls of Gingee these many years after, and shudder to think of a man who would dare them alone."

A figure loomed over the table. Glancing up, startled, I saw it was the man from the steamboat, John Massman. "Maybe I shall join you in building, for I am out of a job. They've sold the boat."

"The *Western Engineer*?"

"Aye. Sold it to a bit of a lass named Majoribanks, or some such name."

Something sank within me. "To Miss Majoribanks?"

72

"That's her." He was sour with the taste of it. "I wanted another trip aboard her . . . she's a good boat . . . but her captain said no. He had his own crew."

"Her captain?"

"Aye, she wastes no time, that girl. She bought the boat and found a crew in no time at all. She hopes to have stores and fuel aboard and be gone within hours, and if I know men, that Macklem will have it done. He looks a slave driver to me."

"Macklem?"

"Aye. *Captain* Macklem now, with sailing orders for St. Louis and points west."

Massman sat down.

My eyes turned to Jambe-de-Bois. There was no triumph in him, no I-told-you-so. There was just disappointment . . . and fear.

Miss Majoribanks was going west on the *Western Engineer* with Macklem for captain, going to the rescue of a brother who might well be a prisoner of the same bad lot who crewed her vessel!

CHAPTER 10

Jambe-de-Bois shook his head slowly. He was scowling. "Too late now. Macklem is a charmer. If he's talked to her, you'd get no place arguing against him. In fact, if you tried it, he would be all smiles and friendly, and when you got out of her sight, he'd kill you."

"Maybe I am not easy to kill."

Jambe waved a hand. "That was what Sam Purdy thought, and Macklem destroyed him."

"I shall call upon her."

"You'll do no good. She's found a man who will take her where she wants to go, he listens to her, and he tells her she is right to go west. He needed a way, and now she's made it easy for him and his crew. You cross them, and they'll kill you."

"Nevertheless, I shall go to see her."

He glanced at the clock in the tavern. "It is close to one o'clock. You cannot go now."

"In the morning, then."

Needless to say, I slept not at all that night and was up with the first light. I say I slept none, yet certainly I must have, in snatches here and there. With the first crack of dawn, I was having coffee, and, without waiting for breakfast, I went out upon the street.

Two men leaned against the hitching rail. One was a man with a stocking cap on, the other wore a black slouch hat, and both were husky, capable-looking men. Yet I merely noted them and turned toward town.

As I did so, one of them called out. "Wrong way, mister. If you're huntin' work with timber, go the other way, toward the boat docks."

"Thanks. I have business uptown."

They were walking toward me, spreading out a little as they came. "You better go to the boat docks. Nobody wants to see you uptown. Fact is, we was warned most partic'lar that you shouldn't go uptown."

I smiled pleasantly. "I suppose you'd stop me if I tried to go?"

The man with the stocking cap grinned. "Why, now, we wouldn't wish for you to get into trouble, would we, Pete?"

"We surely wouldn't," Pete said. "He might have notions of callin' on a certain young lady. Wouldn't do, no way."

"Well," I said, "I suppose you're right. I might as well go back and eat breakfast."

"There! I told you he was smart, Pete! Didn't I tell you? I just said to you, 'That boy's smart. He won't need to be told no second time.' An' what did you say?"

"I said we should teach him a little lesson. Sort of impress him."

My three steps had taken me close to them. I put my right hand up to hitch my collar into better position, and I threw the punch from there. Now I was always taught to punch *through* what I was hitting at, as though my target was the back of the head instead of the chin.

My family runs to heavy muscle and bone, and I'd helped it along with much boxing, wrestling, and hand-to-hand practice, and years of handling heavy tools. I threw my high hard one at the man with the slouch hat, and he never even got his hands up.

He was on my left, and I threw that right high and across. Without losing momentum, I just let my natural shoulder swing carry me and came back with a left that caught Mr. Stocking Cap coming in.

I'd have been surprised if either of them got up, and I was not surprised. Feeling suddenly cheerful, I turned and went uptown.

Penn Street had a row of elegant houses, but I'd not come unprepared, for before coming out onto the street I had put on my tailored black suit. It was one I'd had made in Montreal on my last visit, and it was beautifully styled.

The house toward which I'd been directed was a fine-looking mansion, and the man who opened the door bowed me in when I asked for Miss Majoribanks. I wasn't certain she'd be up.

"Oh?" she looked surprised when she saw me. I don't know whether it was just me or the handsome black suit. "Oh, Mr. Daniel! Do come in!"

A very pretty blonde young lady came through the door behind her, and she said, "Helen, this is Mr. Daniel. He was with us when we came down from Maine."

"How do you do?" Helen had big blue eyes, which she widened very effectively as she took my hand. "We are just sitting down to breakfast. Won't you join us?" She turned. "Daisy, set another place for Mr. Daniel."

The dining room into which she led me was a handsome room with walnut panels and furniture, the table set better than any I'd seen since I left my grandfather's place.

"Helen," Miss Majoribanks' features were stiff, "I'm afraid you misunderstand. Mr. Daniel is . . . I mean he's not . . ."

"A gentleman?" I suggested. "Isn't that a matter of opinion, Miss Majoribanks? Have you ever found me to be otherwise?"

Her cheeks were flushed. Obviously embarrassed, she said, "I mean . . . I did not *invite* you here. This is the home of a friend. I cannot presume to—"

"Invite a laborer? A man who works with his hands?"

I held out my hands to Helen. "Are they so bad, these hands?" I smiled at her. "Is it so bad to shape wood, to build?"

She took my hands, laughing. "Why, they're wonderful hands! And so *strong*-looking! They make me shiver."

Miss Majoribanks' lips tightened a little. "I'm sorry. Had it been my home I—"

Helen held my right hand by the fingers and led me to the table. "Sit here. Please do! Daisy, Mr. Daniel is a big man, and I'm sure he's very hungry."

It was a pleasure to sit at such a table again. Yet despite its richness, it lacked a little something one might have found in my grandfather's home.

"Are you staying in Pittsburgh long, Mr. Daniel?"

"That depends." The coffee was strong and hot. "I came here hoping to build boats. Perhaps to build one for myself for trade on the western waters. But certain things have happened . . . that's the reason I came here this morning. I had to speak to Miss Majoribanks."

"To Tabitha?"

It was the first time I had heard her name. Tabitha Majoribanks. I couldn't decide whether I liked it or not.

"Is it personal? Must I leave?"

"No, no, it's business." I put down my cup. "Miss Majoribanks, if you will permit me. I understand you have bought the steamboat *Western Engineer*?"

"Yes, I have. It was going for a very reasonable price, and it seemed much the simplest and easiest way to go west."

"I'm sure it is. You have a crew?"

"Of course. Colonel . . . I mean Captain Macklem has taken care of all that. He's very efficient."

"And so handsome!" Helen exclaimed.

I paused, not sure how to proceed. Tabitha Majoribanks looked at me expectantly. "This Colonel Macklem," I said, "is the man who killed Sam Purdy."

"Who had first attacked Colonel Macklem."

"No doubt. I was thinking of the manner of it. Also, he was on the road in Maine when Foulsham, the young British officer, was killed."

Tabitha Majoribanks knew where the conversation was going now, and her eyes were chilly. "And you, Mr. Daniel? Were you not on that road also?"

"Yes. I was. But Foulsham was alive when I found him."

"And did he accuse Colonel Macklem?" Her tone was cold.

"No, but—"

She stood up. "Mr. Daniel, I have no idea what you hoped to gain by coming here, nor what you wish me to believe. But if you are jealous of—"

"Jealous?" I remained seated. "And why should I be jealous? What reason could I possibly have?"

Her cheeks flushed, and her eyes narrowed to pinpoints. Oh, she had a fine anger, this Tabitha Majoribanks! And when angry she was remarkably handsome, too. Beautiful was not quite the word at the moment.

I got up then, and before she could speak, I said quietly, "You believe your brother has come upon something important to your country. Mr. Foulsham was pursuing a man, or at least investigating one, who had betrayed his country, a notorious adventurer.

"At this moment, a certain Torville is recruiting all the riffraff he can find, with a view, we believe, to seizing the Louisiana Territory. Colonel Macklem, with a considerable group of riffraff, is now going aboard your steamer. If your boat is the easiest way to the western lands for you, it is the same for him . . . for them."

"You are accusing him?" Her eyes were furious.

"No. I have not sufficient evidence. What I am suggesting is that you find another crew. Find one known to local people, and a captain known to local people."

"You have not sufficient evidence! I should think *not*. All you have is supposition and your own dislike for him. I'm sorry, Helen, but I can no longer remain in the room with this man."

"I'm leaving." I turned to Helen. "I am sorry. I had information. I hoped she would listen, but I did not mean to disrupt your breakfast."

She walked to the door with me. "You will come again, won't you? And please . . . don't take offense. I have never seen her so angry before. She must like you a great deal."

"*Like* me? She detests the ground I walk on."

Helen laughed. "I doubt it. It was what you said about no reason for jealousy that really burned. Do come again, Mr. Daniel."

"Call me Jean," I said. "That's really my name."

I walked back slowly, turning the whole affair over in my mind.

My efforts had been useless. Now she was angry, and if I was any judge of people, the last thing she would think of doing would be to rid herself of Macklem. I had really made things worse, for all my good intentions.

Macaire. I must warn Macaire.

Suddenly, I was alert. I must move with caution. Those two men who'd confronted me outside the inn had not been there by accident, but obviously to prevent me from doing just what I'd done. Only I'd made a proper mess of it.

Macklem, or somebody close to him for whom he was acting, certainly believed that I knew more than I did. No doubt, he suspected I could go to them with concrete information, and wished to prevent that.

Butlin was loafing on Water Street, obviously watching for me. He sauntered along toward me. "Looks like you had trouble," he said.

"No trouble," I said.

"But a man at the inn said you were jumped by two thugs."

"Oh, that!" I grinned at him. "That was nothing to what I ran into when I tried to warn Miss Majoribanks about Macklem."

Briefly, I explained. Butlin stood quiet, listening. He was a good listener, Butlin was, and a man who remembered, but above all, as I was learning, he was a man who knew how to act on what he had learned. Many men have information, but few know how to use it to advantage.

"So what do we do now? Jambe-de-Bois is worried."

"I want to talk to Macaire. Find him for me, will you? I shall change clothes."

My room was quiet. From my window I could see the *Western Engineer*. From my packsack I got out my telescope and studied the steamboat.

A man was standing on a skiff painting over the ship's name. Several men were walking up the gangway carrying boxes and bales. Macklem was wasting no time.

A wagon pulled by two horses had drawn up near

the gangway. The back of the wagon was covered with a tarpaulin, and as I watched, several men surrounded the wagon, all of them facing out. Six husky men came down the gangway. The back of the tarpaulin was lifted and one long box taken out, then another and another.

The husky men took the boxes up the gangway at a trot, and all the while those other men were looking, watching, wary as cats.

A warehouse and big stacks of lumber shielded them from Water Street, and only my position on the second floor of the tavern with my telescope gave me a chance to see it happen.

As I watched, I counted aloud: "Three, four, five . . . six, seven . . . eight." And there were more. At least ten of those long boxes, and nobody needed to tell me what they contained, for I had seen such before. Each box contained at least a dozen rifles. Perhaps more.

There was a light tap on the door, and Butlin came in. Handing him the glass, I indicated the wagon with its tarp, now pulling away. Another was pulling up, and it was unloaded in exactly the same way.

"Well?" I said.

He glanced at me. "Rifles?"

"Of course. There must have been at least a hundred on that first wagon."

"So we can guess, a modest estimate, no less than two hundred rifles aboard—and probably more. That's a lot of firepower."

"Did you find Macaire?" I asked.

"Nope," answered Butlin. "He's not around. At least not yet."

We were silent. The second wagon had discharged its cargo and moved away. Now there was only the usual activity around the hull of the dragon boat.

"What are you going to do?" Butlin asked.

There was nothing I could do. Tabitha Majoribanks would not have me aboard, and I certainly would not serve under Macklem. Whatever was to happen would happen soon, for their boat would likely pull out for the West in a day or two.

"Nothing," I said, "but hunt a job."

Butlin dropped into a chair and stared thoughtfully out the window. "That's a fine girl," he muttered, "a fine, proud girl."

Something inside me cringed. I felt a shame come over me. Yes, she was all of that. I remembered the set of her shoulders, the look of her back as she walked away from me. But I knew she had no use for me, and although she was a fine, proud girl, she also had a fine, devil of a temper.

I said as much. Butlin chuckled. "Would you have it otherwise? If you're going to have steam in the kettle, you've got to have fire in the stove."

Through my telescope, I saw a man walk up the gangway, pausing at the rail. It was Colonel Macklem. My fists clenched.

But fists were not the proper weapon for him. If a man was to tackle Macklem, he must do it with a calm mind, for I knew that man was thinking. He was thinking all the time.

And every thought was of how to kill you, how to make you suffer.

CHAPTER 11

At the boat yard I had no trouble. Boats were building. Men were needed. Timbers were cut in a sawmill, but many needed added shaping, and I was a better than fair hand with ax or adze.

I was hired on the spot.

That afternoon, John Dill, my boss, walked over to where I was working and kicked the chips I'd cut from a timber in facing it. The chips were almost uniform in size, and the timber as smooth as if polished.

"You're good," he said quietly. "Have you built boats?"

"I am a shipwright," I told him. "I have built three schooners, a barkentine, and several brigs, along with a number of fishing crafts."

"I thought so." He watched me work for a time. "Have you built bridges?"

"Several . . . and barns, as well."

"We've a steamer to build. One hundred and twenty-five feet overall, main deck, cabin deck and a texas."

I leaned on my ax. "You will build it here?"

"I shall. If you'll have the job, it is yours."

"You mean I shall be in charge?"

"I've watched you work. You'll do it. I want the job done by a man who loves his work, who loves the wood he works with and the tools he uses."

It was what I wanted. It was what I had come west to do. Now it was here. One hundred and twenty-five feet would make a handsome craft, and once I'd put one in the water I could write my own ticket.

Why did I hesitate?

"Let me give you my answer tomorrow. I must think of what must be done and what I have to do."

"Well enough. You know where my office is. Come along when you've made up your mind."

For a moment longer I waited, thinking, and then once more I went to work, liking the clean, neat strokes of the adze, the way the chips broke away. This was what I had started to do in life, to build, to build boats that would carry the commerce of this wild land, go up its farthest rivers.

When I finished my day, it was dark. I stacked my tools and turned away from the river toward the hotel. If I was going to stay in Pittsburgh, I must find new, less expensive quarters.

There was the faint scuff of feet on the street ahead of me. I stood very still. I'd had a bit of trouble on the previous day, and hoped for no more.

Hands chest high, whether to block a punch or lead one, I continued my walk.

"John Daniel?"

It was Macaire.

"Macaire! We need to talk," I said.

"Aye," he answered. "Come sail with us. You can ship aboard us in any capacity you like. Or you can come as a passenger, as a free trader."

"You speak for yourself, Macaire. Neither Macklem nor Miss Majoribanks would allow it."

"If I speak for you, they'll take you. Will y'come, lad?"

"I cannot. Your Miss Majoribanks thinks I am common stuff—and dislikes me into the bargain. As for Macklem, he's a very dangerous man. We'd kill each other within the week."

"Ah, you don't know him, lad. He's a canny one. He's a way about him, smooth as a French tailor, and he'd say naught against you. In fact, and this will surprise you, lad, he suggested it."

"Macklem?"

"Aye. Your name was up. I don't know if it was Tabitha who mentioned it, or whether 'twas Macklem himself, but your name was up. She said you'd been companions all the way down, and he come out with it, quick and easy. 'Have him aboard,' he says, 'in any capacity he wishes.' The words I speak were his own."

I considered that. Now why should he have me aboard? Obviously, to be watched, and then done away with when the chance presented itself.

"No," I said. "I will not come, Macaire. You're a good man, and I would stand beside you in this trouble, for there's trouble acoming, whether she believes it or not."

We were walking alone on the street. "She kens the lot," said Macaire. "She knows better the trouble than any of us. You know too little of the lass, John Daniel. She knows what's ahead, and well she knows it."

"But—"

"Lad, her father was a canny man. He had those who knew writing to him from all about. The lass knows more than the both of us."

I could only stare at him. "You cannot mean that."

"Aye. Mean it I do. And well I mean it. Do not underrate her, lad. She's got a canny head on her pretty shoulders, a canny head. She's like her pa . . . only more, lad, more."

We walked the rest of the way in silence. At the tavern door, I said, "Come for a dram."

"No. I should be at her side."

He left me then, and I walked inside and went aloft to my room. When I lighted the candle, Butlin was there, resting easy in my chair.

"How did it go, then?" he asked.

"Well enough." And then I told him of the chance to build the steamboat.

"From John Dill himself, is it? Aye, he's a knowing man. You'll find no better anywhere about. He's been up the Mississippi, and he's sailed on the lakes."

"Aye?"

"He helped to build the *Accommodation* some ten years back, at Montreal. He worked on the *Swiftsure* and tried to buy a piece of the *Walk-in-the-Water* before building began. He knows boats, and he believes in steam."

The names were familiar to me. All were Great Lakes steamers, and there'd been a time when I thought of going down to Sackett's Harbor to work on the American steamer *Ontario*.

"Well," he said at last, "you have what you wanted. It is surely your chance, and with a good man, a solid man. If you do this one well you'll have a future, lad, for he has the name of seeking out good men and keeping them by him."

Then I told him about Macaire and what he had

said of Miss Majoribanks. He did not seem surprised.
I said as much.

"Talon," he said, "I have known of Miss Majoribanks for more than two years, and Macaire is right.
There's no shrewder person in the country than her."

"But she's just a girl!"

He chuckled. "Oh, sure! That's all she is, a girl.
But she has a head on her shoulders that is older and
wiser than many a man twice her age. You forget
she grew up at her father's knee, helping with the
business, often making decisions, handling the writing. Believe me, her pen is known to a hundred men
west of here, and they'd die for her.

"You can tell her little about Torville that she does
not already know."

Peeling off my shirt, I bathed in the basin, dumped
the water out of the window, and filled the basin
again from the white pitcher. It was cold, but it felt
good on my arms and chest. When I had dried off, I
put on a fresh shirt.

Butlin had been watching me, and when I had the
shirt on, he shook his head. "You're strong," he said.
"I have seen some mighty men in my time, but never
one with muscles like you have."

I shrugged. "My family runs to muscle. And when
a man lifts heavy timbers morning until night, he'll
become strong or he'll not last."

I looked around at him and said: "Did you ever
lift a twelve-by-twelve that's ten feet long and green
timber? You'll not find too many who can do it once,
but I've lifted them, balanced them, carried them, and
fitted them in place. Not once but a dozen to twenty
in a fair day's work, along with smaller stuff."

Later, at table in the common room below, I said,
"If we do the steamer, I'll be needing help. Will you
work with me?"

"Thanks . . . but no."

"It will be no timbers as big as those I've mentioned," I said.

"It is not that," he said, "but the lass."

"Miss Majoribanks?" I could not call her Tabitha.

"She will need help. She knows what it is she faces, but she will not quit. She will find her brother, alive or dead, and if dead, she'll find where the body lies. You can be sure of it."

I shifted uneasily. The food was being put before us, but suddenly I was not hungry.

"What are you to her?" I asked.

"I am nothing. But they have asked me to go."

He left me then. I felt relief that he would be going with them.

Suddenly I realized that it had been some time since I had seen Jambe-de-Bois. I had seen nothing of him, in fact, since the morning before.

I inquired of the desk clerk about Jambe-de-Bois, but he had seen nothing of him either. I went upstairs to my room.

Glancing from the window, I saw lights on the deck of the steamer.

Undressed, I got into bed, clasped my hands behind my head, and considered building the steamboat and the problems it would entail. Yet through the thoughts of building, costs, time, and materials, her face kept appearing, laughing, angry, contemptuous, cool . . . but always her face.

Disgusted, I sat up. What was the matter with me? Why should my thoughts continually revert to *her*?

Suddenly, there was a tap on my door—the faintest of taps, almost as if it wished not to be heard.

CHAPTER 12

My hand reached for the pistol that lay on the table. A moment of listening, and the tap came again.

It was very late. Sliding quickly from bed, I drew on my pants, tucking the gun behind my belt, and I stepped to the door.

"Who is it?" I asked.

"Macklem," a voice answered.

Right hand on my gun, I opened the door with my left and took a quick step back, drawing the gun as I did so.

Macklem stood there, filling the door. He stepped into the room, lithe as a cat. Noticing my pistol, he chuckled. "Afraid?" he said.

"Careful," I replied quietly, "just careful."

"You have talked to Miss Majoribanks," he said, "and I gather there was some disagreement."

"Of a sort," I said, committing myself to nothing.

He drew back a chair and sat down. "Can we have a light?"

"The candle is there," I pointed with the muzzle of the gun, "if you wish it lit, then light it."

He did so. The match flared briefly, the wick caught, the flame lifted up.

"You do not trust me," he said, as if sorrowed by the fact.

I chuckled. "Not even a bit."

He waved a hand. "No matter. Regardless of that, we need you."

"We?"

"All of us. Miss Majoribanks, Macaire, Mrs. Higgs, and I. We are going west, into unknown country, Indian country. You have had experience with Indians. Macaire says you understand rough country, that you've dealt with Indians. I've come to ask you to join us."

He smiled at me.

"Also," he added, "Miss Majoribanks would feel safer if you were along."

"Did she say that?"

"No," he admitted, "but I sense it. Whether you know it or not, she believes in you. She trusts you."

I grunted.

"I do not joke. We have far to go, and beyond St. Louis, who knows what awaits us."

"I'm sorry," I said. "I have an excellent offer to build a steamboat here. It is what I came west to do."

He was silent for a few moments. "You are a Canadian?" he asked suddenly. "From Quebec?"

"I am."

He hesitated again, as if uncertain how to proceed. "We need a man of your skills," he said. "On such a trip there is much danger and often a need for repairs. Miss Majoribanks wishes to go up some of the unknown rivers, and there will be no boat yards there, nor any skilled workmen."

"I would have thought," I said, "that the men you have with you there would have various skills."

"There's also the matter of companionship," he suggested. "You are obviously a man of intelligence, of breeding. You work with your hands, but you're cut from a higher class."

"What do you know of my class?"

He waved a hand. "It is obvious. You are a gentleman, a man of culture and background. It is in your bearing, your style, your manner of speech. You are most certainly of French ancestry, but not completely so."

"Not completely so," I agreed. "And you, Colonel

Macklem? What is your ancestry? Your breeding? I do not find it so obvious."

He looked up suddenly, and the glance he shot at me was not pleasant. I had touched a nerve, a point of extreme sensitivity. It was a thing to remember.

"Does it matter?" He stood up suddenly, so suddenly that I took an involuntary step backward. It irritated me, for he noticed and was amused. "What matters is that we must have you with us. What inducement can I offer? A chance to trade for furs? To look for gold? To become suddenly rich in some other way? You seem to be a fighting man—"

"I?"

"You." He looked across the table at me. "We understand each other, you and I. We are both men of the world. To the west there are vast lands, free for the taking. There are estates to be had more vast than anything the feudal lords of Europe could dream of."

He looked at me.

"To build a boat is all very well, but to own a thousand square miles . . . every inch of it yours . . . that is something! Fortunes await the strong, and land is there for the taking."

"One day I shall go west but when I go it will be to trade, not to conquer."

He shrugged. "As you will."

His face was half in shadow now. "I think you are a fool," he said abruptly.

For the first time, I thought him a little uneasy.

"Goodbye then." He held out his hand. I almost took it, but I should have had to shift the gun to my left hand.

"Goodbye, and my best wishes to Miss Majoribanks. By the way," I said casually, "did you know that Simon Tate rode east with a message from her?"

He froze. "Tate? Who is Simon Tate?"

"He owns the inn where we met. He is quite influential in a political way. He rode off in great haste."

Macklem left and closed the door behind him. I barred the door and went back to bed. Yet for several hours, I remained awake.

I dozed.

There was a quick rap on the door. I got up and unbarred it.

Jambe-de-Bois was there in his greasy cloak, his long hair straggling about his face, his eyes wild.

"They've gone! You let them go!"

Swiftly, I turned to the window. It was dawn. Where the steamboat had been, there was nothing. The dockside was empty, and on the river there was no trail of smoke.

Something sank within me. They were gone. *She* was gone.

CHAPTER 13

"You do not know him! He is a devil that Macklem! A devil!"

I had never seen him so disturbed.

"What could I do? I went to her, and she would not listen. He was here last night, and—"

"Macklem was *here*? To see you? Oh, my friend!"

When I told him what Macklem had wanted, he nodded his head. "Of course! He has her, her boat, and he has Macaire. Once he gets you, the slate will be clean."

"What slate? What are you talking about?"

"Who can connect him with Foulsham? You. Who is going west after Charles Majoribanks? His sister. If Charles does not escape, the sister does not get back.

Macaire, in whom she has confided, does not get back. And then if Macklem gets you—"

Irritably, I brushed it off. "You assume too much. We suspect much, but we know nothing at all. I cannot for certain connect him with the murder of Foulsham. He was in the vicinity, but so was I. And so were you."

Jambe turned abruptly. "He did not remember me," he muttered. "Or if he remembered, he didn't care! What could I do? Of what could I accuse him without in turn accusing myself?"

"Let's have some food," I said, "some coffee, at least."

We went downstairs and sat at a table in the corner from which both the doors to the street and the kitchen were visible.

Jambe placed his scarred fingers on the edge of the table, and I looked searchingly into his eyes. "You know this man, Jambe-de-Bois. What is it you know?"

"Too much!" he said. "He is a fiend! I am a bad man, *mon ami*, but I am not an evil one!"

"There is a difference?" I asked ironically.

He nodded seriously. "Much difference! Much! Sometimes one is bad. One steals, one kills when fighting, one takes a ship here and there, but what one does is done in heat, it is done sword in hand against other swords, pistol against pistol, fist against fist. You are a fighting man. You understand this?"

I nodded.

"I am bad, *mon ami*, but I am not evil! I am a thief. But never have I killed just to be killing! Never have I held in contempt a human life! Never have I tortured, never have I abused the helpless!

"I am not evil as Macklem is evil! He is cold, vicious, without heart or scruple. He kills to be killing, with no anger but only contempt. He despises men, and despises women even more. The girl . . . . Miss Majoribanks. He hates her most of all!

"Yes, I know him. But I do not think he now knows

91

me. At first . . . well, I was afraid. I, who have feared nothing, fear him.

"But I was younger then, without this beard and this gold ring in my ear, with two strong legs.

"He has been what he is from a very young child. He was so in the slums, yet his beauty of body won him attention. He was given a chance. He was taken into a wealthy home and educated, yet when the time came he tortured and killed his benefactors. He escaped to sea. He betrayed his ship, stole the money, went ashore, and took a new name.

"He has betrayed, defiled, ruined, and always with an easy smile—with laughter even. And many times he has been on the verge of great wealth, but always something defeated him.

"We came ashore on an island in the eastern waters, came ashore with treasure for each of us to share. Four of us to bury it, and Macklem brought a lunch and several bottles of wine.

"We drank the wine. I drank little because it was food I wanted. I stole meat from the basket, and when I thought I'd been seen, I threw it quickly down. Later, where the basket had been, I saw a rat . . . a dying rat, kicking its life out . . . poisoned.

"Turning, I ran back down the beach. All were drinking, most were drunk. When I shouted at them, Macklem turned deliberately and lifted a pistol to shoot me.

"Oh, I was young then. I had two strong legs, and I turned and dove into the brush. The bullet cut a leaf above my head.

"I ran and ran . . . he did not follow. Behind me I could hear the screams of the other two men, dying. He had poisoned them both.

"For three days, guarding our boat for himself, he hunted me. Twice, knowing I would be hungry, he left poisoned food upon the beach. Traps. The rats and gulls died, but not I. Finally, he left."

"And the treasure?"

"He was no fool. He took it with him."

It was a terrible story.

"After seven long months I was picked up. Since then I have heard of him often. Several times I have seen him, though he does not recognize me. I have searched for him, followed him, waiting for the moment when I might see him die."

"Yes, Jambe, I understand," I said.

"But he does not die. With any weapon he is a master. I have never seen his equal. Believe me, *mon ami*, do not provoke him. He will kill you."

"I am not so sure."

"You may be sure. And this is the man with whom you have left Miss Majoribanks. This is the man!"

"By steamboat it is thirty-five days to St. Louis. Say he cuts the time to thirty."

"So?"

"Overland, with horses, say it is six hundred miles. With average luck, twenty-five days, with the best of luck and fresh horses along the way—good horses —perhaps ten, fifteen days."

His fingers gripped my wrist. "You mean it? You will go?"

As we ate I considered all aspects of the journey before us. We must cross at least six hundred miles of rough country, and the distance was only a guess. Much would depend upon my horses, the weather, stream crossings, and the fortunes of the day. If we were lucky, we could do it with time to spare.

I placed gold coins on the table. "Buy food. The simpler the better. We will want coffee and what can be easily packed and prepared. I must see Mr. Dill."

Dill was in his office, and I wasted no time, nor did I keep anything to myself. He was a solid citizen, a respected, worthy man, and I told him exactly what the problem was, even about Macklem and what Jambe-de-Bois had told me.

"Go," Dill said, "and luck to you." He got to his feet. "This is my country, too, young man, and much of our future depends on the development of the Louisiana Territory.

"I've dozens of horses, and you'll need strong stock." He stepped to the door of his office and motioned to a clerk. "John, go to the stables and have Joel put lead ropes on Sam and Dave. Mr. Talon here will take them."

By mid-afternoon we were across the river and headed west. I was glad. The fever of the West was again upon me.

Yet what Dill had said remained in my mind. He had said this was his country, too. Was it mine? By birth I was a Canadian, but now I was here, and was this not my country also?

Traveling was no new thing for me. On the Gaspé Peninsula of Quebec where I was born there was not much work. My family owned much land there, but to work as a shipwright demanded long trips. Several times I had been down the coast to the towns of Maine. I had worked in Nova Scotia. My first trip to Toronto had been with my father and uncle while I was a very young boy. We had worked all summer at Lachine, near Montreal, building several *bateaux*. These were forty feet long, eight feet wide, with almost vertical sides and a blunt bow and stern. We built the sides of fir, the bottom of oak. These boats were occasionally sailed, more often rowed or poled, and when close in shore, pulled by men walking in shallow water, near the shore. Later we helped build one of the first Durham boats to be used in Canada. These were eighty to ninety feet overall with a beam of ten feet, and were usually sailed or rowed. They could carry thirty-five to forty tons of freight downstream, eight to ten tons upstream. Both types of boat were much used on lakes and rivers in Canada.

My father had helped to build the *Toronto Yacht*, working on it in 1798 and 1799 for several months. In its time she was the sleekest, fastest craft on the lakes, and when she was wrecked in 1812 he had been very unhappy.

He was a man proud of his work, taking great care in the shaping of every timber, and every craft built by his hands always remained in his heart. He had come home to Percé, disappointed and angry. He had been asked to work on a twenty-two-gun ship being built, but after seeing the design he refused.

"They are fools!" he told my mother. "Fools! She will never stand a rough sea. They do not know the lakes, these men. They think we have a lot of mill-ponds here. And the timber! Much of it is not seasoned, but they will go ahead."

"And we needed the money," my mother said.

"Aye!" he muttered gloomily, "but I will have no part in a thing badly built. Men will die because of it, but regardless of that, a man does not waste the trees it took God centuries to grow in building something of no account.

"Remember that, my boy," he rested his hand on my shoulder. "The wood with which we work has strength, it has beauty, it has resilience! If it is treated well, it will last many, many years! If you build, build well. No job must be slackly done, no good material used badly. There is beauty in building, but build to last, so that generations yet to come will see the pride with which you worked.

"There are proud ones who look with disdain upon a man who works with his hands. Do not do so. It is not every man who can shape a timber or build a bridge or ship. Work with honor, my son, and build with beauty and strength."

We brought our *bateau* down from Lachine on that first trip and tied up at Allan's Wharf, which some people were beginning to call Merchant's Wharf, at the foot of Frederick Street.

It was always a good day when my father reached Toronto for at some time during his stay he would enjoy a drink with Dr. Baldwin, an Irishman who knew much of building, and he often came to watch when my father was building a squared-log house. Such houses demanded the master craftsman, for each log must be precisely squared and shaped. My father was such a man.

We rode until sundown, then changed horses and rode on until midnight. We camped in a forest of towering trees, gathering broken branches for fuel, and at daybreak we were off again. At noon we switched horses again. As evening came on we stopped in a meadow, watered and curried our horses, then turned them loose to graze.

The roads and trails were dry, the weather cool. We had no trouble. Several times we stopped at lonely farmhouses and once at an inn in the village.

For seven days we rode hard, stopping now and again to sleep and rest the horses, eating when we could find the time. We came on the morning of the eighth day into a little hollow where a small stream ran southwestward through a meadow. It was an area where the forest was thinning out, the big trees growing fewer and fewer.

Jambe-de-Bois pulled up beside me, easing himself in the saddle. "Stoppin'?"

"For a piece of time. We could all do with rest."

He was as ready as I was, and we rode through the water of the creek into a small grove along its edge. Hidden by brush and the overhang of the trees, we swung down, stripped the gear from our horses, and picketed them behind the trees in a corner of the meadow.

Jambe-de-Bois stretched out on a grassy slope in the shade of an elm, and I walked off a bit, picking a few berries left on the bushes. Doing so, I drew near our trail, although I was concealed from it by thick brush.

Suddenly I heard the hoofs of approaching horses.

"Wait!" someone said.

"There is nothing. I can see for several miles. They are further ahead than we thought." It was the voice of another.

"We'll come up with them tonight . . . and it must be tonight, Jem. You know what the colonel said. And I'd cross the devil himself sooner'n him."

Now I could see.

There were four men. One rode a fine dapple-gray gelding. He was a thin, raillike man who could have weighed nothing, but he had two knives in his belt and long, tapering fingers that kept dropping to the knives with a caressing touch.

I could not see his face, nor the face of one other. There was a burly, red-haired, and dirty man with greasy buckskins, and also a man in a black slouch hat and homespun pants who had a wide grin but few teeth. There was a bend in his nose and a scar on his eyebrows. He looked like a man hunting trouble.

Standing very still, I waited. Then I inched my hand to my gun and drew it. If they should happen to see me, I'd shoot without warning, instantly. The shot would also be a warning to Jambe-de-Bois.

But they didn't. They moved on. Fortunately, none of them noticed where we had turned off. On down the trail they went.

"Jambe?" I spoke softly as I approached him. "Get the horses. We're moving out."

He groaned, sitting up. Briefly, I explained, and he went at once for the reluctant horses.

"What now?"

"That way." I pointed.

"But there's no trail!"

"That's right. There is no trail. We'll make our own." I checked the pistol I carried, then my rifle.

"Jambe?" I described the men. "If we see them, don't wait, don't talk. Shoot them on sight."

CHAPTER 14

St. Louis was bathed in moonlight when we finally arrived, crossing the river on a flatboat we happened to see making ready on the east bank. We landed at a dock well away from the streets, which was just what we wanted, hoping to arrive without being seen.

We rode through the dark streets, taking nothing for granted.

On a side street we found a man leading a team into a barn. A lantern hung over the door, another inside.

"Is this a livery stable?" I asked.

He was a well-set-up man of perhaps fifty. "No," he glanced at us, then at our horses. "However, I've got some empty stalls and a corral. Cost you two bits a day down at one of them stables in town. I'll board the lot of them for a dollar a week."

"You've got yourself a deal."

We dismounted, stripped our gear from the horses, and carried it inside. I handed the man a dollar.

"We want to put up at a quiet place," I said. "Know a good one?"

"Sure do. Mary O'Brien's. Ma, we call her. She lives right down the street. Fourth house from here. Her husband was lost on the river, and her boys have gone down to New Orleans. She's a fine woman, and she can use the money."

The house was sparsely furnished with homemade furniture, except for a big old chest of drawers. It was neat and everything was spotless.

When I commented, her blue eyes twinkled. "Mister," she said, "I got nothing else to do but clean. I sew a mite, but there's little enough of that to do, and my sewing's not fancy.

"Board and room, two dollars a week for each. I know that seems expensive, but folks are crowding St. Louis right now, and grub's expensive. Why, sugar's gone to thirty-five cents a pound, and coffee's fifty cents!"

"That's mighty expensive, ma'am," I agreed.

I handed her four dollars. "That's the first week," I said, "and we're good eaters."

"Like to see a man eat hearty. Does my heart good."

"Now tell me, Mrs. O'Brien, if I wanted to go some place where I could hear the news, where would it be?" I asked.

"Choteau's." She paused a moment, looking from Jambe to me. "On the other hand, if you was listening for the kind o' talk that leads to no good, I'd say Pierre's. It's only a few step beyond the corner, and he's an honest man."

"We'll go along then. And could we bring you a bit of something, Mrs. OBrien?"

"Go along with you. I'll set up with my bit of coffee."

Pierre's was a place of wooden tables and benches, and Pierre was a stocky man with a healthy stomach hanging over pants cut off below the knees, and a wide belt that struggled to retain the stomach.

The place was empty except for Pierre. For a few minutes we talked in French, then Pierre reverted to English. "It will be the only tongue soon. It's an American land we have now. Once there were French wherever a man looked, up the river and down. Now there's few of us left except for trappers and a few traders."

He glanced from Jambe-de-Bois to me. "Jean Daniel Talon. It is a good name. There was a Talon once who was a pirate, I think."

"Aye," I said dryly, "he was the first of our line, and might be better able to face what we have before us than we. There's a steamer coming up the river. It used to be the *Western Engineer*."

"The sea serpent?" He chuckled. "I fancied that one! I'd like to have owned her myself. What's she called now?"

I shrugged. "We came overland to get here first." Then I outlined the story for him, and when I finished, he looked carefully about.

"I am an honest man, so they tell me nothing. But I can hear, and I hear a great deal. Men have come to St. Louis, and they have disappeared inland . . . a few at a time, maybe fifty or a hundred in all.

"There are rumors something is in the wind, but there are always such rumors. I believe none of them."

"You're empty tonight?"

He scowled. "Yes, and I don't understand it. Most of the time there's twenty-five to thirty men in here. Of course, it's late."

I got up. "Pierre, we're tired and we're going to turn in. We'll be at Mary O'Brien's if there's news, but tell nobody where we are."

We left. At the corner we paused a moment. It was cool. A gentle wind was coming up the river carrying a faint suggestion of woodsmoke.

Jambe-de-Bois looked around impatiently. "It's no good place," he said. "We'd best be getting on."

Yet I hesitated a moment longer. Had that been a shadow in a doorway? I reached inside my coat for the pistol, rested my hand upon it. Slowly then, I turned to follow Jambe.

They came out of the darkness with a rush. Only a whisper of moccasins on the boardwalk. They were already hidden in the shadows waiting for us, and they closed in fast.

My pistol came out, and I fired. There was no chance to miss, the man was almost within arm's length to me when the gun went off. He stopped in full stride, and then he fell.

A sweeping blow with the barrel of the pistol dropped another one, and then I jammed the muzzle of the pistol into the throat of a third.

Jambe-de-Bois had turned like lightning. I never dreamed he could move with such speed. He was laying about him with a knife. There was a picket fence adjacent and we turned to face them there.

Somebody struck the knife from Jambe's hand, and it went flying. As I lost hold of my pistol and they closed in, I saw Jambe fall back on the fence. He struck out with his fist, then stooped suddenly, and, when I fought myself clear of those closing in on me, Jambe was laying about him with his wooden leg!

Catching a man by the throat with my left hand, I lifted him clear of the ground and shoved him into the face of another. Then I rushed them both off their feet, taking a savage blow to the kidney. Turning with a sweep of my hand, I struck a man along the temple.

Another charged in low, and I brought a knee up into his face, slamming down on the back of his head as my knee came up. He grunted and fell, his nose crushed.

I took a wicked blow to the face. A dozen men struck at me, it felt like, and then I was hitting, driving at them, punching low and hard. I butted one man in the face, kneed another in the crotch. And suddenly there was a breathing space, and we stood alone, gasping for breath.

Yet not quite alone. At least three men lay on the ground around us, one of them the man I'd shot.

Jambe-de-Bois held to the picket fence with one hand, his peg-leg in the other.

"There must have been a dozen," I said.

"Seemed like it, but I figure only nine," he said complacently, "and they weren't much. In the old days at sea, they'd have lasted no time at all."

The dark street was empty. Pistol shots at night

were no new things in St. Louis, where drunken trappers on their way home often fired their guns just out of sheer good spirits.

With my toe I rolled over the man I'd shot. He was dead, all right, and he was one of those I'd seen following us west. Near him lay my gun. I picked it up and thrust it into my belt.

One of the men, badly hurt, started to rise. Jambe-de-Bois hefted his peg-leg. "Lie still, damn you," he said conversationally, "or I'll smash your skull."

The man ceased to move. Jambe-de-Bois rolled him over on his back. "If you live," he said quietly, "don't let me see you again, or I'll split you open like an overripe melon."

He strapped on his leg. I watched him, wondering how many times before that leg had come off in brawls. It made a terrible weapon, and, whatever else he was, Jambe-de-Bois was a mighty fighter. With him around—and on my side—I need never worry about my back.

We limped home. Somehow I'd been kicked on the leg, although I didn't remember it, and when I looked into the mirror in my room I found a welt on my cheekbone and a lump over one eye.

Jambe-de-Bois dropped on his bed and stared at me. "You look to have been fighting, man," he said and chuckled. "Best fight I've had in a year! But you did us a service, a real service when you shot the first one."

"You think so?"

"Aye. 'Tis my thought that he was the leader and the paymaster as well. When you downed him, it took the heart from some of them, for they were not sure when they'd be paid . . . if ever."

"I couldn't miss," I said. "He came right at me."

For two days we loitered about, each going his own way, each listening. We heard nothing. It was true that men had appeared, bought lead for bullets, powder, bought food and disappeared from sight, but nobody knew anything substantial. Or, if they did, they preferred not to speak.

At night we avoided troublesome places and retired early. I tried to see Choteau, who observed even more than Pierre, but he was out of town.

Late one morning there was a light knock on the door. It was Mary OBrien.

"It is Pierre," she whispered. "Come!"

He was in the kitchen, with a cup of Mary's coffee.

"The steamboat," he said low voiced, "has come. It is about four or five miles up the river, at a small island off the mouth of Coldwater Creek. A boat has come down from the steamboat to the town and has landed at the mouth of Mill Creek."

"Who has landed?"

"Two gentlemen and a lady. They are on the street now."

Tabitha was here. She was in St. Louis. Would she listen to me now?

CHAPTER 15

At my suggestion, Jambe-de-Bois kept himself hidden at Mary O'Brien's. At a nearby corner I paused, getting my bearings.

Choteau was the man I most wanted to see. It was around his fur-trading establishment that the town revolved. Whatever was happening, he would know. Perhaps he had returned by now.

Despite the hour the streets were crowded, and most of those on the street were men, trappers in buckskins, traders from back East or from New

Orleans, a mixed lot, but all rough, capable, enduring. There was excitement in the air, for the very thought of what lay beyond the wilderness, the unknown lands of mountain and plain, generated such excitement.

I saw no familiar face and walked along toward Choteau's. In my belt was the pistol I still carried, Foulsham's pistol. At my belt, the knife—a knife from India that had been in my family for many years. It had been taken from the castle of Gingee by my famous ancestor. It was a knife of steel such as I had never seen elsewhere, a knife with an edge like a razor.

Tabitha was here . . . the steamboat upstream, at an island off a creek mouth . . . no doubt hidden there.

St. Louis was sure to be filled with Macklem's supporters, the men of Baron Torville. The town itself had a population, Pierre had told us, of between three and four thousand, yet during the season when the traders were gone upstream, when others had gone down to New Orleans with cargos, the population might be trimmed to no more than half . . . this was a guess, yet those gone would be the best of the fighting men.

What would Torville's plan be? He would need money. The logical way to that was to intercept the shipments downstream of the winter's take of furs.

He would need trade goods for presents to the Indians, for however many men he could recruit they would be insufficient unless he could also win the Indians, or some of them, to his side. There were malcontents among them as among our own people, and the chance of scalps and loot might be enough. The streets were dusty and crowded. Wagons drawn by mules or oxen, men riding horses, Indians of several tribes, men of all nationalities, and dozens of dogs. I stepped back against the face of a building and looked left and right, scanning the faces in the crowd, the buildings opposite. I had an uncomfortable sense of being watched.

The pistol in my belt was a reassurance, yet my greatest reliance was in my own physical powers. Somehow, when in trouble, I often forgot that I even carried a weapon.

After a moment I went on, checking out various stores and shops along the way. I entered several, looked around, watching the street as I did so.

Two men had come up the street opposite the store and stopped there, leaning on the hitching rail and talking. From time to time they stole quick looks at the last store I had entered.

Standing at a counter I bought tobacco, which I did not use but which Jambe-de-Bois would enjoy and, paying for my purchase, I walked through the gap between the counters and to the back of the store. There was an entrance there through which wagons were loaded and unloaded. I went out, closed the door behind me and walked swiftly along back of the buildings, stepping around stacks of old lumber refuse, and piles of wood for winter burning.

Choteau had returned.

He was in his office when I entered, and he turned to study me. As to where he placed his loyalties, I did not know for sure, but I had no choice but to explain fully. Quickly, I told him that Charles Majoribanks had stumbled upon knowledge of a plot to seize the territory, that Tabitha Majoribanks was now in St. Louis on her way west to find him, and that I suspected Colonel Macklem to be one of the plotters.

"I am a fur trader, not a politician," he replied. "I know nothing of the situation you outline. There have been several abortive attempts to seize Louisiana, one way or another."

"The steamboat has several cases of rifles," I explained.

Choteau tipped back in his chair, rubbing his chin thoughtfully. Then he shook his head. "I do not know you, Mr. Talon. I do not know you at all.

You're a very young man who has come to me with a somewhat fanciful tale, that is all."

"You have met Charles Majoribanks?"

"He was entertained in my home when he came in on the *Western Engineer*."

"You did not entertain him on his return? You did not see him then?" I asked.

"No, as a matter of fact, I did not. It was my understanding that he remained upcountry for the purpose of studying plants and animal life."

"You have not heard from him since his first visit?"

He shrugged again. "Should I have? I do not see all who pass through St. Louis."

He studied me thoughtfully. "You might think on this, young man. Colonel Macklem has been in St. Louis several times. He is well thought of here. He has many friends. He is well known along the Missouri River. We have had no reason to complain of his conduct."

He paused, shuffling some papers upon his desk. "Another thing. I believe you underrate the capabilities of Miss Majoribanks. I must inform you that she is an extremely astute young woman, both in trade and international politics."

I was surprised. "I did hear," I admitted, "that she was well spoken of. . . ."

"You heard correctly, sir. Miss Majoribanks," he said dryly, "was trained in a very thorough way by one of the shrewdest minds in the country. I hope she will see fit to call on me while here."

For a moment I had nothing to say, and suddenly all notions of plots began to seem rather childish. Yet one thing remained.

"You do not think it strange that the steamboat did not dock at St. Louis? That it proceeded upstream to what is, in effect, a hiding place?"

He frowned momentarily. "Yes," he admitted, "that does seem a bit strange. But no doubt they have their reasons."

"And Foulsham was murdered while carrying information about such a plot?"

"I know of that only from you. I have no reason to doubt your word, but on the other hand, many men are murdered while traveling."

He got to his feet. "It has been pleasant, Mr. Talon, but I have other duties. You will excuse me?"

I went out and stood in the store, watching the people, yet thinking of everything else. Was I a fool then? How much, really, did I know?

Macklem was known here, and he was liked. He had, if he was a plotter, laid his groundwork very well.

Suddenly, I thought of my own situation. What was I doing here? What had prompted me to leave a good job—one in which I might soon have become owner or part-owner of a steamboat or a boat yard —and come off to this far place?

I felt like a fool, a colossal fool. I should have stayed in Pittsburgh, building boats.

"Quite an odd lot, aren't they?"

Startled, I turned to see a young man beside me, a slender, rather handsome young man with a nicely boned, aristocratic-looking face. He indicated the passers-by. "I wanted to see this. I had to see it. Now that I see it, I find it hard to believe . . . the redskins and all."

"This is their country," I commented ironically. "You should expect to find them here."

"Oh, but I did! I expected it. I knew they would be here. Why, we used to play Red Indians when I was a child in England, but to know I am here is something different."

He turned and extended a hand. "I am Donald McQuarrie. I am trying to get on with one of the fur companies . . . with Choteau, if he'll have me."

"My name is Talon," I said.

He nodded. "So I was told."

"Told?" I stared at him.

"Mr. Choteau told me who you were, what you looked like. He said I should talk to you."

"I am not a fur trader. I've no jobs to offer," I said, "and my meeting with Mr. Choteau was very brief. I do not believe he was much impressed."

"On the contrary." McQuarrie watched the crowd, his eyes alert and busy. "The Choteaus have been around for a long, long time, Mr. Talon, and will be around for a longer time still. There's talent in the blood, and a good deal of native shrewdness.

"You see," he paused, "I'd been to see him just before you, and about much the same thing."

For a moment what he said did not register. "Much the same thing?"

"I followed you west, and, I might say, had a devil of a time at it. When you travel, you do not waste time. You just about succeeded in losing me a couple of times."

"You followed us?"

"You . . . yes, I did. You see, when Simon Tate reached Boston, I was there. The gentleman to whom he went on arrival was a friend of mine, and I had let him know why I was in America. He let me see the papers Tate had, and Tate told me of you, so here I am."

"Might I ask why?"

"Obvious, is it not? I want Macklem. I want him very badly indeed. Most of all, I want Torville."

"There is a connection then?"

He glanced at me. "Of course. You see, we don't like Torville. He's a dangerous, completely unscrupulous man. He has betrayed the French, and he has betrayed us. He has no loyalty but to himself. Now he is here."

McQuarrie was quiet, sincere. He talked well and he made sense of a kind, yet I did not trust him. But then, I am not usually a trusting man, and inclined to be wary of strangers. This one was apparently British, and he had that manner that one recognizes as a product of the better schools, and we saw a lot of that sort of thing in Canada. Many of our most and least successful pioneers had been retired British officers.

"I know you no more than Choteau knew me," I said.

"I am a brother officer of Captain Robert Foulsham. In fact, he was a year or two ahead of me in school. We were on the same mission, actually."

He glanced at me. "Ever hear of Lord Selkirk?"

"Of course."

"He established a colony west of the Great Lakes, if you'll recall."

"I know the story. It was attacked, some said by the Indians . . . I have forgotten the details. But wasn't it nearly destroyed?"

"It was. And although he never appeared at the site, Torville was responsible. He was one of those who stirred up the trouble. The Hudson Bay Company wanted no settlers coming into the area who might interfere with their fur trade. As it was, they had complete control. Then Selkirk entered the picture. Yet there might have been no trouble had it not been for Torville, who wanted no settlers there either, and for his own reasons."

"What reasons?"

"Think. The fur cannot last forever, and when the fur trade is no longer profitable, the Hudson Bay Company will relinquish its authority. Into that vacuum a man of will, authority, and determination might step."

"He's mad!"

"Perhaps . . . but uncommonly shrewd as well, and he knows how to use the passions, discontents, and greed of other men. Our belief is that he has support from quite a number of wealthy, power-hungry men in both Europe and America. Until such time as your army has posts and forts in the territory, there will always be those who will plot to seize it."

Suddenly, a thought struck me like a thunderbolt. What if Tabitha's father, with his chain of correspondents, had been one of those backing Torville? And if he had, did Tabitha know or didn't she?

I was facing McQuarrie, who was about to speak.

"What a small world, after all!" The voice was cynical, amused. "Tabitha, will you look now? It is the young man from the trail! The one who was going to remain in Pittsburgh; I wonder what brings him to St. Louis?"

I turned around.

It was Macklem. And beside him, Tabitha.

CHAPTER 16

Tabitha extended her hand. "It *is* good to see you!" she said, and, surprisingly, I thought she meant it. "Are you shopping?"

"Sightseeing," I said. When I thought of McQuarrie, and turned to introduce him, he had vanished in the crowd.

"You seem surprised," Macklem said.

"I am surprised."

"We're only going to be here today and tomorrow," Tabitha said. "We've some suppplies to buy and I want to see if there's any news of Charles." And then she added, "Colonel Macklem has been helping me."

"He looks like he was born for the job," I said, and felt better when his features tightened.

"Where Mrs. Higgs?" I said.

"She's aboard the boat," Tabitha said. "She wasn't feeling well."

"I am so sorry. Perhaps I could go and see her," I said cheerfully.

"Oh, but you can't," Tabitha said, "the boat is—"

Macklem interrupted. "She's not well," he said. "She's not receiving visitors."

"Another time," I replied.

Just then a man came up and touched me lightly on the sleeve. "Mr. Talon? Mr. Choteau would like to see you. When it is possible."

Tabitha stared at me, coldly curious. "Talon? I thought your name was Daniel?"

"Jean Daniel Talon," I said.

Macklem's attention had sharpened. "Talon? I know that name."

"It is possible," I said, then added, "please give Mrs. Higgs my regards."

"I shall," Tabitha said. Suddenly she turned to Macklem. "Colonel, I must see Mr. Choteau myself. Shall I meet you at the dock then? In two hours?"

He was caught completely off guard. I think he had no intention of letting her out of his sight, that he had planned to carefully manage her trip ashore so that she talked to no one when he was not present. The sudden suggestion caught him unprepared.

"Can't we do that later?" There was irritation in his tone. "I mean, there's much to do, and—"

"Do what you must, Colonel. Mr. Talon will escort me, as he is going to see Mr. Choteau himself. Mr. Choteau's will offer me the best choice of things I need for myself and Mrs. Higgs. So, then . . . in two hours?"

Abruptly, she turned her back on him and took my arm.

I chuckled.

"You must have ridden very fast," she said.

"Yes. We did. I wanted to get here before you."

"Why?"

The question stopped me. Finally I said, "Because I thought you might need help, and I wanted to be near if you needed me."

"That was sweet. You know, Mr. *Talon*, you can be very nice at times . . . and very obnoxious at others."

"Then we are two of a kind," I said dryly.

She laughed.

"Have you news of your brother?"

"No." She was suddenly serious. "That is one reason I wish to see Mr. Choteau."

We were shown into his presence at once. When he saw Tabitha, he bowed deeply. "This can only be Miss Majoribanks?"

"How do you do?" She accepted the chair he held for her, then looked up at him. "Is there any word of Charles? Anything at all?"

"Nothing. I've sent some scouts up the Missouri and up the Platte. They will make inquiries. The last we heard of him he was on the Kansas River, gathering plants."

"I must find him."

He fussed with the papers on his desk. "You must not think of it. Stay with us in St. Louis, Miss Majoribanks. We will find him. It is a vast country out there, so vast you cannot even imagine it, and looking for a needle in a haystack would be a simple task by comparison."

"Nevertheless, I shall go. Charles, if he is not injured, will find *me*. He will hear of our steamboat— and surely there cannot be two such in the world. And he will come to it—if for no other reason than to dispose of his plants. I'm certain he will come."

"If he is free," I said.

She turned sharply. "What do you mean?"

"Charles may have been captured by enemy forces," I replied. "Only that."

"And what is your interest in this?" she asked suddenly. "You're not even a citizen of the States. You are a Canadian."

"We're all Americans, I think," I said quietly. "But I have asked myself that question. I am a man who believes in order. A stable government is the responsibility of all men and women everywhere.

"Revolution, for whatever reason, is self-defeating, for violent revolution results in violent reaction. Oddly enough, the worst reaction usually comes from within the revolution itself, and the first casualty is the revolutionary. Look what has happened in France, for example. Those who created the revolution, those leaders of revolution, all were victims of it. And who reaped the benefit?—Napoleon.

"Peaceful change is the healthiest change, but if you will look closely you will see what the so-called revolutionary who deals in violence wants is simply violence. He is unhappy with himself, believes himself incapable of coping with the situation as it is, so tries to disrupt it. He wants violence to relieve his own anger and pent-up hatred."

"But does he not claim to be acting for the people?" Mr. Choteau suggested.

I shrugged. "The 'people' is an abstraction. It is one of those general terms that has no meaning in fact. For 'the people' is in reality many peoples, with many interests, many possibilities. It is always interesting to me that none of these persons who claim to act for the people have ever consulted the people themselves."

"And this Baron Torville?"

"An adventurer, pure and simple. One of those, no doubt, who still lives in the thinking of William the Conqueror or those Normans who invaded Sicily and set up a kingdom there. He is as out of date as the dinosaur, sir, but does not realize it."

Choteau looked at me thoughtfully, and I think Tabitha was surprised as well. As a matter of fact, so was I.

"You seem well-informed, young man."

"No, I am not. But history was much discussed at our table when I was a child, and the events of far-off nations seemed to us as if they were next door. He who started our family lived much in Asia and the interest in history and the people of history remained with us all."

"You were fortunate. But these ideas? On revolution, and revolutionaries?"

"When a man works or travels he can also think. I have had much time to think, less time to talk."

"And what do you believe is the end result of it all?"

"Some innocent people are killed, occasionally some of those who might have been sympathetic to the cause, much property is destroyed, often property that would have been very useful to the revolutionary government had it succeeded, and in the end a Napoleon appears who is tougher, stronger, and more determined than those who were thrown out.

"Of course, most revolutionists do not . . . really . . . want change. They simply want to sit in the driver's seat."

I paused. "You wished to speak to me, Mr. Choteau. What can I do for you?"

"You are going west. It suddenly occurred to me that you might be better armed. I do not know what weapons you have, but I'm sure you have nothing as fine as what I have here.

"It happens that a young Austrian of great wealth came here to hunt buffalo. He wished also to kill a grizzly bear. He brought excellent weapons, much equipment . . . and then became ill.

"This was months ago. Now he has sent word to sell his weapons and equipment. Since you are going into such dangerous territory, I thought you might be interested."

"I am definitely interested."

He stepped to the door. "Jacques? Show Mr. Talon the Pauly rifles, will you, please?"

I followed Jacques.

When the door closed behind me, I wondered if Choteau was not equally eager to get me out of the room so that he might talk to Tabitha without being overheard. But in any event, I had no excuse to remain, and the guns did interest me.

Jacques was envious. "I should like to own them,"

he said, "but I have not the money. It is very much, very, very much!"

"Tell me who made them."

"Pauly was a Swiss, from Bern or near there, and he served in the Swiss army, then moved to France. At a demonstration before one of Napoleon's generals, Pauly fired twenty-two shots in two minutes."

One rifle felt especially good in my hands, a slender, graceful weapon.

"That is a weapon Pauly made for the young gentleman. Made it with his own hands, and it is beautifully done."

"Did Napoleon try it out?"

"And approved it. However, it was too expensive a gun for an army. See? You open the breech with this lever and put in your cartridge. It uses less powder and will not hang fire, and it can be loaded or unloaded at great speed."

I was impressed.

"And here are two Collier pistols, with handturned cylinders."

They were going to cost me more than I could afford, but how much is a man's life worth? I hesitated, then held the rifle in my hands while I considered, and was reluctant to put it down. It had a nice feel, moving easily to the shoulder. The sight was good. At last, I put it down.

Taking up the pistols, I studied them. The Collier had originally had a sort of mechanism to turn the cylinder as the gun was fired, but it had not proved satisfactory. Yet turning by hand was simple enough, and gave you several shots without reloading.

"How much?" I said at last, knowing they were too expensive.

"You will have to talk to Mr. Choteau. They are at his disposal, and from what I hear, he can put upon them what price he wishes."

Reluctantly, I left the guns and walked back to the office. Tabitha was gone.

"Where is Tabitha?" I asked. "She must not go back to that boat!"

"You will see her tonight. She has only gone to my home. We are to have a small, informal reception for her this evening, and we would be pleased if you would attend."

"I shall."

"You like the guns?"

"Beautiful!" I said. "But beyond my possibilities, I think. They are perhaps the finest I've seen."

"Yes," Choteau leaned back in his chair, "they are excellent weapons. As a matter of fact, the price was left to my judgment, for to the owner money has no meaning. He is more concerned that the weapons be properly used."

To that I had nothing to say, so I turned the conversation. "Will Colonel Macklem be present tonight?"

"Of course. Do you object?"

"Certainly not. It is your home. He will be your guest. Whatever differences we may have, they will not be settled in your home."

"Thank you." He paused. "Now, as to your plans?"

Plans? I had no plans except to keep Tabitha out of trouble; to interfere with whatever revolution Torville had in mind; and then to get back to building boats.

I told him as much. Choteau chuckled. "I'd say you had your work cut out for you, Mr. Talon. Have you ever been in a fight of this kind, Mr. Talon? Torville will have some of the Indians with him, you know."

"I've nothing against Indians. Grew up with them."

Choteau got up. "It is growing late, Mr. Talon. Come in tomorrow when Jacques can get out ammunition for you."

"I don't believe I can afford those guns, Mr. Choteau."

"Mr. Talon, the guns are yours."

CHAPTER 17

At Mary O'Brien's I changed into my dark suit. Jambe-de-Bois stared at my preparations with obvious disapproval. "It's no good thing you do. Stay clear of the man and give him no idea of how you move or where."

"I've got to warn her. Somehow I've got to make her get rid of him."

"Huh! You tried that, lad, and it came to nothing. The man is a charmer and a devil. He'll have her won over now, and you'll be shut out colder than ever. I say—don't go."

There was sense in what he was saying. Even as I arranged my cravat, I knew he was right, up to a point, but I was determined to see Tabitha, and little else mattered.

There was a belligerence in me, too, a need for crossing swords with him that drew me on. Wary as I was, I was also filled with a kind of savage eagerness when near the man. Never before had I so wanted to fight someone; never had I deliberately courted trouble. But there was something about him I wanted to smash. And he probably knew it and felt the same.

"Midnight," I told Jambe-de-Bois, "no later. I shall be back, and in the morning I will go for the guns. Then we will go up the river, for we have things to do."

"I like none of it."

"Rest easy . . . and if you see an Englishman about, one named McQuarrie, tell him to stand by."

"Aye," Jambe-de-Bois said gloomily. "If I see him, and if I see you. Protect yourself. I'll not say protect yourself in the clinches for there are no clinches with Macklem. He'll destroy you at long range. Destroy you."

"You worry too much."

I put my hand on his shoulder. "Rest easy, I say. I shall be back at midnight."

The street was dark and empty when I stepped from the door, pausing a moment on the porch to look right and left. There was a faint smell of rain in the air.

I had only a short distance to go and decided to walk by the river. Stepping through my gate, I closed it behind me and started walking. I had not walked far when I thought I heard a faint, despairing cry.

Instantly I stopped, listening. Again I heard it. Listening, I waited.

No sound.

I continued walking, disturbed by that cry. Should I try to help? I was dressed for company.

I paused, then was about to continue when I heard the cry again.

"Please! Help me!"

The call seemed to come from the water off the stern of the keelboat nearest to me. Leaping over the bow, I ran along the walk toward the stern. The faint cry came again. I bent to look over into the water.

At that instant there was a rush of feet behind me. I tried to straighten and turn, but a glancing blow from a club hit me on the head, my hat went flying, and, dazed, I tried to get my hands up.

There were at least six of them, and they all had clubs. Only their numbers saved me, as all of them crowded for blows. I staggered and fell against the bulwark with blows battering my head. Badly hurt, I tried to fight back. But the pressure of their bodies forced me back, and with one wild, despairing grab

I clutched the collar of the man nearest me and went over backward into the water.

Down, down I went, the other man struggling wildly, first to strike at me, then only to break himself free. Somehow I'd caught a deep breath before I went under, and I clung to him, taking him with me. I surfaced, saw the flash of a gun, and something rapped my skull. Down I went, losing my grip on the man, but clinging to his collar.

Desperately, I struggled, and when I came to the surface I was some distance downstream, trying to swim and cling to something at the same time.

My skull bursting with pain, I surfaced. Something huge and black loomed over me, and then I knew nothing more.

The motion was easy. Sunlight lay across my bunk, across the Indian blanket on which my hands lay. I could see my hands and the slow movement of light that was one with the gentle motion.

For a long time, I just lay and watched the light move toward my hands, touch them, then slowly move away. The rhythm was hypnotic. I watched it, dully conscious of my comfort, aware of nothing.

Something bumped near me and my eyes moved. They moved of their own volition, for there was no will. Now they were looking at the source of the light.

A round hole in the wall . . . a porthole. I heard another dull thump, then a voice. "Still alive?"

"He's alive." It was a girl's voice. "Still unconscious, I reckon. His pulse seems stronger, though."

"We shouldn't have taken him from St. Louis, Pa. He might have had kinfolk nearby."

"Doubt it. Though he was dressed rich. Some folks surely tried to kill him."

The talk came through the open port, but it meant nothing to me. I simply lay still, and my eyes had returned to the light on my hands.

Then I smelled something. It was a good smell, a rich smell, a smell of cooking.

Cooking . . . food.

Food?

My eyes blinked, my muscles stirred, and I hitched myself up in the bunk. I could hear movements. Slowly, awareness came to me. I was in a clean, well-blanketed bunk, on some kind of boat. Not a very big boat, for the deck was right above my head and the bottom was right below me.

What boat was this, and where was I? Who was I? I considered that for a minute and then said aloud, "Jean Daniel Talon."

A voice exclaimed, and the curtain over the door drew back.

A girl stood there, a very small girl with a very tiny figure, dark hair and eyes—very serious eyes now—and parted lips. She was pretty, very pretty.

She wore a fringed buckskin skirt and a calico blouse. She had moccasins on her feet.

"You're awake!"

"Either that, or you're a dream," I said.

She blushed. "You're awake," she said dryly. "Now you're hungry, no?"

"Now I am hungry, yes," I said. "But first, tell me where I am, what boat this is, and who you are."

"You're on the Missouri River. This is my father's keelboat, and I am my father's daughter."

"How did I get here? What happened?"

"You were hit on the head several times. Two cuts, many abrasions and scratches. You were shot . . . a furrow through your scalp. You can part your hair in the middle now, if you like."

"How did you save me?"

"We were coming upriver, not stopping in St. Louis. We heard some yells, some scuffling, and a shot, and then we saw a bunch of men on the end of a boat, and not long after that we saw you in the water. I reached over and grabbed you by the collar.

"Pa kept going and I held on. When we hit a straight stretch of river, Pa lashed the rudder, and he come for'rd and helped me pull you in."

"That was last night?"

"That was five days ago, come suppertime."

"Five days!"

Tabitha would be gone. The steamboat would be long gone. My friends would think me dead.

"You saved my life, and for that I thank you, and I thank your father."

She canted her head on one side and looked at me. "You are hungry now? You must be hungry."

"I am ravenous. I could eat you."

She made a face. "I am not edible. Nor would my father like it. I am his crew."

"You? You're too small!"

"I am *not!*" She stuck out her chest. It was a very nice chest. "I am strong! I am formidable!"

"And I am hungry. We decided that."

"And I am sorry! At once!"

I put my head back on the pillow and looked up at the underpinning of the deck. It was good work, done with nails, of course. I prefer pegs and fitted joints. Nails, well, they are a convenience, but for fine work . . .

There were heavy steps on the deck, and a man came down the ladder and stopped at the bottom, his hands still on the ladder, staring at me.

"Huh! You do not look so bad awake," he said. "What are you?"

I rolled onto my elbow. "A hungry man wanting a meal. I am also a man who was banged on the head. It still aches."

He chuckled. "You have some stitches. My daughter, she sews well, huh?"

"She stitched up my head?"

"What would you have us do? Leave flesh and hair hanging over your ears? But no . . . it was not so bad. But some stitches were needed. They will come out some day. Do not worry."

"How far are we from St. Louis?"

He shrugged. "Far is a question always? How far?

On foot? By keelboat? By horse? And how much of a hurry is it?"

"I left some people there, and I want to pick up some guns."

"You are in no shape to ride. Even if you had a horse."

"I have horses in St. Louis."

He shrugged. "Maybe you have a castle on the moon. Both of them are far away, and I am not going back to St. Louis."

"You are not one of Choteau's people?"

"I? I am my own people. We have this boat, Yvette and I. It is our boat. We have some traps. We catch a few fish. We pick berries along the river, and we know where they grow. Sometimes we shoot a buffalo or an antelope or deer. We sell our furs. We are nobody's people."

"Yvette. It is a pretty name."

"It is. It was her mother's name, God rest her soul. But do not you throw sheep's eyes at my daughter. She is my crew. Without her, I am nothing. Without her, I am an old man with an empty boat."

"You are far from old."

"Now I am young. The day she leaves me, that little one, I am old. I shall be old upon the minute."

He walked in and sat down opposite me. He was nearly as broad as he was tall, with wide, thick shoulders and no fat. He had square, powerful hands.

"You tell me now, while she is busy. What was it about?"

"They were trying to kill me. Not to rob me, to kill me."

He brushed that away. "Certainly. I could see."

"There is a steamboat on the river, a steamboat that looks like a great black serpent."

"I have seen it."

"It is owned by a girl, a very lovely girl named Tabitha Majoribanks. She has come west looking for her brother, Charles. She has for captain a man named Macklem. It was his men who attacked me."

"She does not like you, this woman?"

"It is not the woman. It is Macklem, and a man named Torville. They are very dangerous men. Macklem gathers other men somewhere up the Missouri, and he has been talking to Indians. He wishes to take the Louisiana Territory . . . all of it."

He took out his pipe and began to tamp tobacco into the bowl. He paused. "He would take it, huh? He has something to do, that one."

"Nevertheless, he will try."

He looked at me thoughtfully. "You are in love with this woman?"

"No!" I spoke quickly, perhaps too quickly, for he looked amused. "I would help her find her brother, but also it is to defeat this man that I am here."

"Macklem?"

"Macklem, yes, and Torville, too." I spread my hands. "I work with timber, you see? I am a man who likes order."

"You have met this Torville?"

"No."

"Then I have the advantage. I know him." He put the pipe in his mouth and touched a match to it. "I also know young Charles. A good boy . . . a very good boy."

CHAPTER 18

We talked the day away and into the dark hours. Yvette fed us, then made coffee, and made coffee again. LeBrun, who was her father, was an easy man. He was quick to see, to understand.

He had met Torville on his first journey into the Mississippi Valley—and did not like him. He had also met Charles Majoribanks on the scientific expedition. They had made room for him. After all, he was a fine botanist, and that such an aide could be had for nothing was unbelievable.

Charles had made friends. "The Indians liked him." LeBrun explained. "He was often among them, learning from them, for they know much about plants.".

"Where is he now?"

"Who knows? He disappeared. He went up the river and vanished." He paused, lighting his pipe again. "We go to find him."

Slowly, I eased to my feet and attempted to stand up. Yvette watched anxiously; her father simply watched. He knew what I was feeling, knew that a man has things to be done that cannot be done lying on his back in bed.

Shakily, I got to my feet, my head spinning. I tried a step, staggered, caught myself as Yvette started quickly forward, and then slowly sat down again.

"You need rest!" she protested.

"You've been looking for Charles," I said. "Why?"

Yvette flushed a little, then put her chin up. "We like him."

"It is reason enough," I said. "And nothing else?"

"What more is necessary?" LeBrun asked. "He came to us one time, and we ate together, we talked, and he was a good companion. He talked of flowers and trees and things of which I had not dreamed, of how the value of the soil may be judged by the plants that grow upon it."

"He liked my cooking, too," Yvette said.

"I've no doubt that was not all he liked. Even a botanist can have eyes for more than plants."

She blushed. "He was a nice man, a gentleman."

"You have no horse?" I asked LeBrun.

"What need have I for a horse? When I hunt, I do so afoot or from the boat. You would be surprised

124

how often we find our game while it is swimming—or drinking."

"I must have a horse. I must go first to St. Louis to my friends and to get my outfit. I shall need a horse."

"Well," LeBrun rubbed his jaw thoughtfully. "There's some Indians over east of here a mite. They're good folks, mostly, and we set well with them. Might make us a trade."

"Trade? What have I to trade?"

"You got your clothes," he said, "and you've got a mighty fine pistol. And a knife like I never seen."

"I can trade the clothes, but not the pistol, and especially not the knife. It has been in my family for two hundred years."

It was pleasant here, but I was suddenly very tired. I lay back on the bunk and looked up at the deck overhead. Too bad they had to use nails. Those were good timbers, well cut and trimmed, they could have . . .

When I awakened, it was dark and still. I lay very quiet, suddenly alert and listening. There was no sound but a faint creaking of timbers.

It was too silent.

No breathing came from the opposite bed, now hidden behind a curtain. Very gently, I eased back the blankets and put my feet on the floor, feeling for my moccasins. One hand reached for the pistol, drawing it near. Stepping into my pants, I drew them up, drawing my belt tight, listening all the while.

Still no sound but the faint lap of water. There was a vague sense of movement . . . was the keelboat moving? I moved to the steps that led to the deck, if such it could be called.

A keelboat of the smaller size, which this was, was usually about forty feet along and eight or nine feet wide, with both bow and stern pointed. The deckhouse occupied more than half the length, with a steering pulpit aft and seats forward for oarsmen. One square sail was mounted on a mast above the forward part of the deckhouse.

9

Along each side was a cleated walk used by polers in working the boat upstream. Obviously, with only Yvette and himself aboard, LeBrun must depend on the sail for going upstream, the current when going down.

Stepping out on the narrow, cleated walk, I crouched to keep my head below the level of the deckhouse. For a moment, I held perfectly still, listening.

The water rippled, the sensation of movement was more pronounced. We were adrift.

I looked aft toward the steering pulpit where LeBrun should be. No figure loomed against the night.

Very cautiously, I worked my way aft, crouching when I reached the after end of the deckhouse. The small deck in the stern was empty.

Keeping low behind the bulwarks, I reached the rudder. The proper steering position was from the pulpit, but I'd no intention of skylining myself up there, so I raised a hand to the handle and gently centered it.

Where were LeBrun and Yvette? And who had set the boat adrift?

There was no doubt in my mind that it had been deliberately set adrift, but why I could not guess.

Indians? I doubted it.

Had Macklem and his crowd caught up with me? Where were LeBrun and Yvette?

Keeping my left hand on the rudder, I managed to keep the boat away from the banks. From my crouching position, or even standing and merging my body with the rudderpost, I could not see the river ahead.

I prayed that the river was free from obstructions.

There had to be a reason for setting the boat adrift. Had LeBrun and Yvette gone ashore for some reason?

The more questions I asked myself the less I knew the answers.

I crawled into the pulpit, where I could at least see the river ahead and get a better grip on the rudder.

For a moment I gripped it, expecting a bullet at any instant. None came.

I guided the boat closer to the bank, watching for a place where I might run it in close and tie up. At all costs, I must get back to St. Louis.

The river took a slight bend. I headed in close to the bank, grounded the bow, then leaped ashore with the line. I took a quick turn around a sturdy tree, then another turn and a half-hitch, then still another.

The boat secured, I went off into the woods.

I reached a path. For a moment I stopped and listened, then I stepped into the path and walked away from the river, moving carefully in the moonlight. When I had walked no more than two hundred yards, I heard a faint sound.

I dropped to one knee near a bush.

At the same moment I knew that I was not alone. Not more than six feet away, I could faintly see the outline of a head and the whiteness of a face. A man was crouched and waiting.

Whoever he was, he had not heard me come, nor had he any idea of my presence. Suddenly a voice said, "Newt? You hear something a moment ago?"

"Ssh!"

"Newt, I—"

"Ssh, damn it! They're coming."

The second man, whoever he was, must be not more than six feet away.

Then, I saw the second man. He was right in front of me, facing away.

Rising up only slightly, I took a careful step forward. The night was cool, still. I could see him more clearly now. I put my hand on the cold barrel of my pistol, chilling it.

Then I heard the murmur of other voices, talking very low. Yvette and LeBrun! My fingers cold from the gun barrel, I reached out suddenly and touched the bare neck of the man before me.

He leaped like a startled rabbit. "A-a-agh!" he gave out with a choking scream and smashed backward

127

with his gun butt. It missed, but the man ran into the brush.

Newt came out of hiding and onto the path. I had dropped down again, and Newt could see nothing.

He swore viciously under his breath and turned square around to start back. "Looking for something, Newt?" I asked very softly.

He had nerve, I'll give him credit. I was up again. He leaped right at me. I'd no desire to shoot, not knowing where LeBrun and Yvette might be hiding, so I stiff-armed him in the face with the butt of my palm, then clubbed my pistol barrel over his skull. He dropped in his tracks.

Squatting beside him, I took his gun and knife. The gun I slid behind my belt, the knife I tossed into the brush, and then I felt around for his rifle, sure there would be one. The moment I put my hand on it, I knew from the shape and weight that it was a trade musket of the kind sold to the Indians.

I stood up. "It is all right," I said quietly. "One's down and the other one's still running."

Yvette and LeBrun came along the trail then, and I stepped out where they could see me. "They cut the boat loose," I said, "but I tied her up downstream a ways. Shall we get along down there?"

"What about him? Is he dead?"

"Doubt it. He's too hardheaded. But let's take him along. Maybe he can tell us something."

LeBrun caught the unconscious man by the scruff of the neck and jerked him erect. The fellow moved, seemed to come conscious.

"Walk!" LeBrun commanded. "Or *I'll* hit you!"

The man stumbled along, gradually gaining more command of his feet. When we were aboard the keelboat, we took in the line and drifted downstream almost a mile, then tied up again.

With heavy canvas curtains over the portholes, LeBrun lighted a lamp.

The man was a stranger, a surly-looking fellow with

a streak of blood from a broken scalp to add to the dirt and whiskers on his face.

"Your friend's still running," I said, grinning at him. "I just touched him on the back of the neck with a cold hand. Jumped right out of his skin."

"Yeller!" The bewhiskered man sneered. "Yeller clean through. I told Baker he was no good."

Baker. That was one name.

"What do you want *them* for?" I asked, gesturing toward LeBrun and Yvette.

"None of your damn business!" he snapped, and I slapped him across the mouth.

Like I've said, I've a heavy hand. It smashed his head around on his neck and jolted him to his heels, although to my notion, it had not been a hard slap.

"I don't like that sort of talk," I said mildly.

Yvette had started forward, and she was staring at me wide eyed.

"I like the kind of talk with information," I said calmly. "I want to know who everybody is, where everybody is, and what they're planning to do."

He started to make an angry reply, and I half lifted my hand. He shrank away, and I could see he had no particular taste for it. "Do you no good," he said. "He'll kill you anyway. Them too. That's what he told me. 'Kill 'em,' says he, 'I don't want to be bothered.'

"'What about the girl?' I says, and him, he just shrugs. 'Just so she doesn't talk,' he says."

"Who is *he*?" I asked.

"None of your—" I lifted my hand, and he shrugged. "Do you no good anyway. You're dead. You're dead as a doornail. He'll see to that. The Baron, I mean."

"Torville?"

"Who else? He's got over ten thousand men, and he's going to take them soldiers first, and then the rest of you as he moves. We're going to *own* this country. Right up to St. Louis and Santy Fe. You'll see."

"Where is he now?" I demanded.

Suddenly a rush of water rocked the boat, and we heard the low chug-chug of an engine.

"That's him now," the man said, "an' he's got you, dead to rights!"

CHAPTER 19

With a gun barrel against the man's back, I blew out the light. There was moonlight outside, and we lay close under the bank, with branches hanging around us. Unless we had already been seen, there was a chance we might be passed by.

Peering out, I saw it. Huge, black, and glistening, the great eyes of the serpent staring ahead, the smoke puffing from the flared nostrils, the huge fins obscuring any sight of the stern wheel that churned the water behind it.

It was, I had to admit, a fearsome object. It gave off a sense of enormous power, of evil, of mystery.

"I seen her before," LeBrun said. "She mounts twelve guns."

Our prisoner snorted. "Twelve? She's got *twenty* now!"

"What are they doing?" Yvette asked.

"Passing by," I said.

An idea was already working itself around in my head, and we had no time to watch over a prisoner. I wanted him away from us, not knowing what we were doing but frightened enough to be too cautious to signal the serpent ship.

"Remember those Sioux?" I asked LeBrun, who just looked at me.

"Gives me an idea," I said. "Let's just turn this man loose."

The prisoner looked at me sharply. "Let's leave him ashore," I said. "He'll get back to his friends if he's lucky, but if the Sioux need a scalp, they can get his."

"Now see here!" the man protested.

"Get him ashore," I told LeBrun.

Despite the man's protests, we put him ashore. "If I were you," I said low voiced, "I'd be almighty quiet. They're all around us. You be quiet and you might get upstream to where your outfit is. We've got no time to watch over you, and the girl doesn't want you killed. Lucky for you she's soft-hearted, or we'd just let you drown."

He was gone into the brush. We got back aboard. "Cut loose," I said, "and let's get out of here."

"There's a breeze coming up," LeBrun said. "We might make some time upstream before daylight."

"Try it then," I said.

To loosen the half-hitches and scramble aboard, hauling in the lines, took a matter of a minute. With poles we pushed off. The keelboat got into the current, and we slipped away to follow the steamboat.

There was a little wind, and we finally got out of the full sweep of the current losing scarcely a half-mile in the process. We got our sail up, and the keelboat began edging upstream with painful slowness. The steamboat could do a good ten miles an hour against the stream; we would be lucky to do one.

When I took the rudder and LeBrun went below for coffee, I was alone with Yvette. "You said you were going to find Charles. Do you know where he is?"

"We think we do."

"You believe he is in trouble?"

"Yes. When they can use him no longer, they will kill him. I think he knows this."

"He cannot escape?"

"How? There are many men with Torville. They

would track him down and have him at once, and then they would kill. We must find him."

"Macklem's steamboat may find him first. It can travel much faster than us."

"Maybe. Papa does not think their pilot is good, and the pilot *must* be good. There are snags, sand-bars, and sawyers—"

"What's a sawyer?"

"A tree whose roots or branches are buried in the mud at the bottom. It bobs up and down, swings back and forth with the current. They can take the bottom right out of a boat, especially a steamboat, because they hit so much harder. Papa knows this river. He has been on it many times in keelboats and canoes. He says there is no river like it, and he has worked on the Ohio, the St. Lawrence, and the Mississippi."

The wind held strong, and we moved along, gaining a little speed.

The banks were low, thick with trees and brush. In the moonlight through the clouds, the channel was clear, but the current was strong.

Suddenly, I caught sight of something on the water, just ahead. "Yvette?" I whispered, for sound carries far over water. "What is it?"

She looked out. "It's a canoe. There are three men in it."

With our sail, we were gaining, but not very much. LeBrun came out and stood by the rail, rifle in hand. My gun was behind my belt, the butt easily reached.

"They're waiting for us," Yvette said suddenly. "They're paddling just enough to keep going."

It was true, and suddenly a low voice called out, "Ahoy, there! Stand by!"

The voice was one not easy to forget. It was Jambe-de-Bois.

"It's all right, LeBrun," I said. "I know one of them."

His face turned toward me. "I do not," he said

bluntly. "Yvette, take the rudder. Come over here, Talon."

His rifle covered them. "Stand by," he said quietly. "You know *one* of them. We do not know the others." He glanced at me again. "How well do you know the one?"

It was a good question, for how well did I know him?

"Talon?" I knew that voice, too. "This is McQuarrie. Can we board you?"

I passed them a line, to which they made fast the canoe, and drew them in close. McQuarrie scrambled aboard, then Jambe-de-Bois. For all his peg-leg, he came up nimbly enough. No doubt he had boarded many a craft in his day.

The third man then came up, and he was a stranger. A stocky, well-set-up man in buckskins. A mountain man by the look of him.

"Have you seen the black ship?" McQuarrie asked.

"Aye," I said. "She went up the river back there. Skimmed right past us, and lucky for us she did."

"Who are these men?" LeBrun demanded.

Explanations required only a few minutes, but LeBrun kept studying Jambe-de-Bois. "It's you I've seen before," he said suddenly.

"I've never been on the Missouri," Jambe-de-Bois said. "You're mistaken."

LeBrun glanced at the sail. It was bellied out, and the keelboat was moving well despite the current. "Hold to the channel," he said to Yvette. "We'll be up in a minute."

He led the way below, then turned to look at first one, then the other. "Where is it you're bound?"

"I was hunting him," Jambe-de-Bois said, indicating me.

"Hunting him? How could you know he was alive?"

"I knew nothing, only there was talk of a big fight, and I found his hat on the wharf, so I asked around and some said there was a boat passing at the time.

Thinks I, with his luck, he got aboard her. So here I be."

"And you?"

McQuarrie shrugged. "I am a British officer. I have no authority here, but I want Torville. He is a murderer and a traitor."

The buckskin-clad man shrugged. "I am Otis Pinkney. I think you know of me."

LeBrun nodded. "I do. And you're welcome aboard. Make yourselves at home here. It will be dawn soon, and we've a hole to hunt."

"So has Macklem," Pinkney replied. "He'll not want to be seen by daylight on the river, I'm thinking."

There was coffee in the pot, and we shared it. There was beef jerky, and we tried that—almost the last of the beef picked up below St. Louis by LeBrun. From now on, it would be buffalo meat or antelope, and maybe a deer.

"I've something for you," Jambe-de-Bois said when we were alone. "Choteau sent it."

"How'd he know I was alive?"

Jambe-de-Bois grinned. "I lied. I told him you sent me for them . . . the guns, I mean." He opened a sack and took out the Pauly rifle and a brace of Collier pistols.

I took the rifle in my hands. It was what I had wanted. A good, fast-shooting gun. And the pistols. There was ammunition for each of them.

Yvette came to the door. "We will tie up now. Papa needs help."

It was already dawn. In the middle of the river was a large sandbar on which grew clumps of brush among the piled-up driftwood. We moved in behind an island beyond the sandbar, an island covered with willows and a thick growth of underbrush and many trees including wild plum. There, in a position that hid all sight of the keelboat, we tied up to a huge old tree that had beached itself on the island and become half-buried in the sand.

We all were tired. Leaving the cabin to Yvette and LeBrun, the rest of us stretched out on the deck.

When I awakened some hours later, the sun was high and all was still. Everyone else was sleeping. Belting on my pistols, I took the rifle and went ashore, wandering along the edge of the island, close to the brush. There were wild grapes in profusion, and many wild raspberries. Pausing here and there to eat, I also listened for any sound, any movement.

Somehow we must locate Charles Majoribanks and free him, if, as we assumed, he was a prisoner. Next we must locate the dragon ship and keep it under observation. If Tabitha was no longer in command, we must somehow capture the steamboat and take her back down to St. Louis. And, in the process, somehow disrupt whatever plans Torville had—and Macklem, for I was sure they worked together.

The late morning was very still and overcast with clouds. Again I paused. The willows were very thick where I stood. Looking through the leaves I could see several deer at the edge of the water, drinking.

For a moment I stood watching them, for the wind, slight as it was, was from them toward me. I was well hidden, but wild animals will rarely see you if you remain still, and I was watching.

Suddenly, the head of one doe came up sharply, then the others. Instantly, I was alert. Waiting, listening, I heard the faint sound of a paddle in the water, and then a canoe. In it were four Indians—a man, two women, and a young boy.

They came in close, and the man held the bow into the sandy shore while the boy sprang ashore and hauled the canoe higher.

Obviously, they were a family on the move. I walked out from the willows toward them, and they saw me at once, standing very still, all eyes on me. I held my hand up in a sign of peace and spoke to them. "You have come far?"

The man hesitated, then spoke slowly. "Far."

They wore moccasins of elkskin blackened with

135

smoke, with an ornamental seam across the back and flaps turned outward. It was little enough I knew about western Indians, but this I had learned from Butlin, that such moccasins were worn by the Omaha.

I gestured toward the brush. "Many berries. Good." I rubbed my stomach and grinned at them, showing the few I had in my hand.

The women had gone about making a fire. They had chosen a spot up a creek, sheltered from the mainstream of the river by a clump of chokecherry brush.

The boy was a handsome lad, very quick. He kept watching me as I talked to his father. I did not smoke, but I carried tobacco. I offered the man some. He accepted it, and we sat down together.

"You hunt?" I asked.

He gestured upstream. "Much hunt. Buffalo. You see?"

"Not yet." I gestured toward the brush behind me. "My boat is there. Many men. We look for a man." I described Charles, as he had been described to me. "Maybe with bad man . . . bad white man," I added.

He puffed on his pipe.

"Big serpent boat. You know?"

"Black," he said, "I know."

"You be careful," I suggested, "some good men, some bad men with it."

"Bad men," he looked at me gravely, but his eyes twinkled, "make big snake work hard. Carry steamboat on back."

His own name, he told me, was Red Tail. They were going to visit an Indian village that lay on a river I took to be the Kansas.

"Long time ago," he said, puffing on his pipe, "Omaha big people . . . big nation. Much sickness . . . many attacks by the Sioux. We are few now. Maybe ninety warriors.

"It is no longer as it was," he said, the words coming to him as he spoke, "the old ways are gone. Young men no longer make arrows. Now guns."

"It is easier now, with the white man's pots? Easier to boil food? Easier to hunt with his gun?" I asked.

He looked at me. "Easy is not good," he said bluntly.

I got to my feet. "I go back to my people, Red Tail." I held out my hand. "May there always be meat in your lodge."

He chuckled and bade me go well.

He was still chuckling as he walked back to his family, but when near them, he turned and called. "Old camp . . . you go Bonhomme Island. Upstream. Some days away. Plenty men come . . . plenty gun. I think much trouble. Much trouble."

Bonhomme Island. I had heard of it. Walking swiftly, I returned to the keelboat. Rather, I returned to where I expected it to be.

It was gone.

CHAPTER 20

Gone!

I came out of the willows and looked around, unwilling to believe the boat was not there.

My tracks were still upon the sand—and others as well.

There was scuffed sand . . . running feet, no doubt. The line tying up the keelboat had again been cut. A few feet of rope was still tied to the tree and trailed off in the water.

A thought came to me. I ran back through the willows, slowing only when I drew near the camp.

But they had heard me coming, and Red Tail and his son were on their feet.

It needed a solid half-hour of bargaining, and I was lucky at that, but I traded Foulsham's pistol and my shirt for Red Tail's canoe.

He would, of course, make another one before leaving the spot, giving his son a valuable lesson in the meantime. Once the trade was made, I wasted no time. I had always been good with a canoe.

Now, my rifle close beside me, I started upstream, with swift, even strokes, holding to the slack water close to the banks and studying the stream to avoid the main current.

Somebody had captured the keelboat and all aboard. I had seen no blood, no bodies.

I dipped the paddle deep and the canoe shot forward. With swift, sure strokes, I took the canoe upstream at a rate that would have won many a race, but I had always loved a canoe, and this one was light and finely made. Red Tail was an artist, if the work was his.

Before the sun had set, I sighted it.

The keelboat was a good mile ahead. There was only a small breeze, just enough to keep it moving. The sun was going down, but an hour of light remained, perhaps a bit more. Now the keelboat was before me and my time would come.

The last light was slipping away, the banks were casting dark shadows, and here and there a huge old tree leaned above the river like some monstrous hand, waiting to grab whatever came near.

I felt good. The paddling exhilarated me, and I was prepared for anything. My coat had been left aboard the keelboat, and I had traded my shirt, so I was naked to the waist. The night wind felt cool and good.

I heard a peculiar sound. It was a dull murmur, a sound I could not place.

Rapids? A waterfall?

It dawned upon me suddenly. It was a steam

engine, its sound merging with the churning of the waves.

Instantly, I dipped my paddle deep and turned toward the shadows of the shore. Narrowly missing a huge sawyer, I angled across the current, glimpsed a suddenly appearing sandbar, skirted it, then crossed over.

The sound was unmistakable now. The steamer was behind me, coming upstream. It must have detoured into a tributary. It would overtake and pass me within minutes. And ahead of me and them was the keelboat. The steamboat would overtake it before I could.

I reached the shadows of the bank, and, safely hidden behind overhanging branches, I watched the serpent ship come steaming up the river.

Huge, black, glistening with spray, its great flared nostrils puffing smoke and sparks, it charged ahead.

I wondered who was now aboard.

Lights gleamed from her portholes, baleful lights. After it. passed, I moved out from the shore and started forward.

I rowed hard, dipping my paddle with a strength that carried me swiftly forward.

Under cover of darkness, I gained. Now I could see. They were not only side by side, they were in trouble. The keelboat seemed to be trapped, and the steamer, rushing up alongside, had run hard and fast aground.

I wondered if LeBrun, who knew the river as well as any man, had seen the steamboat coming and deliberately led it aground. I wondered if, indeed, he was a prisoner.

Gently, to make no sound, I inched closer, moving alongside a big old tree whose roots—a grotesque, spiderlike snarl of black tentacles—were above water. I could already hear voices. Moving my canoe alongside, I made it fast, tying a slipknot to aid in a hasty getaway.

Then I waited and listened.

Suddenly, a commanding voice, "Baker? Is Talon aboard there?"

"No, he's not. There's the peg-leg, LeBrun, and LeBrun's girl, but there's no Talon."

"Just the three of them?"

"There's a Britisher . . . least he sounds it. Says his name is McQuarrie."

"Ah?" There was cruel satisfaction in Macklem's tone. "So I've got another one of them, have I?"

That accounted for them all but Pinkney. There was no mention of him.

"Stand by then, Baker, and look sharp. As soon as we float this ship, we'll pick you all up. Get a line rigged to tie on. We'll tow you upstream."

"With that stern wheel?"

"It will make no difference, man. We'll just run out a good line. Stand by now, and look sharp."

Something stirred in the water near me. It was no time for shooting. I drew my knife and held it low, the cutting edge up.

The steamer's engines began to turn over, and the great stern wheel threshed powerfully at the water, in reverse. There was no movement.

My eyes waited for whatever it was that would now take place.

Suddenly, during a lull in the frantic efforts of the steamer to dislodge itself, a low voice spoke, "Talon? Is it you? Pinkney here."

"Come in slow," I said, "I've got knife enough to float your guts on the river."

He came in slow, hands up, rifle aloft. It was him, all right. Nimbly, he got into the canoe, and I sheathed my blade.

"Well, there they are, lad," he said, calling me lad, and him not more than four or five years older. "We've got our work laid out for us. What had you in mind?"

"To take the keelboat and the steamer."

"We were captured. LeBrun took a rap on the skull. Later, when I saw it was no use, I ducked behind the cargo forward and when the chance came, went over the side."

Softly I explained what Red Tail had told me about the camp on Bonhomme Island.

"I know it well," Pinkney said.

He crowded close, whispering so softly his voice was almost lost in the rustle of water. "On the steamer? Is there anyone?"

"I can't be sure of any but Macklem. I hope there's Macaire, for he's a good man, the very best, in fact. And I hope there's a man aboard there as a hand name of Butlin." I didn't mention Tabitha.

"You don't say? Old Calgary there? That shines. I know him . . . know him well. We trapped a winter together on Lake o' the Woods, far to the north. Sold our furs in Pittsburgh."

"We've got to take the keelboat," I whispered, "free McQuarrie, Jambe-de-Bois and LeBrun. Five is better than two.

"Let's go." I was suddenly through talking. "Let's go now."

He pulled the slipknot, I dug in the paddle, and we shot away from the snag and toward the keelboat. We had come close by when somebody aboard the keelboat saw us.

"Hey? Who's there?" he called.

He sputtered, then pitched from the keelboat into the water. There was a loud splash, and Otis Pinkney said, "Move in close to him, lad. I want to get my knife back."

"Your knife? What—?"

"Not bad, for the distance and the dark," Pinkney said complacently. "Of course, we were moving in on him all the while."

We touched the side, and I took a turn around a kevel and threw a couple of quick half-hitches. Pinkney was already aboard, rifle in his hand, knife in his teeth.

I followed.

Two strange men came toward me. "Get below and turn 'em loose," I said to Otis.

"What about you? There's two of them."

"It's nowhere near enough," I said, and moved in fast. I had it going for me, of course. They weren't expecting trouble until one of them saw the breadth of me, which wasn't like anyone aboard. He started to speak, and I swung the Pauly rifle butt around with my left hand. It caught him alongside the head with one solid *thunk*, and he hit the deck with another. The second man was no yellowbelly. He came at me.

He was already in close, so I brought my fist up in a good stiff uppercut and his head snapped back like it was on a hinge. I don't think he'd ever been hit that hard before. His feet left the deck, and he hit the boards in a sitting position.

It was no time for polite work, and at that moment I was impatient. I swung a neat kick to his chin and went on across him toward the others who were coming.

Somebody on the steamer yelled, "What's going on over there?"

Four men were coming at me, and I'd no time to reply. I wanted to save my shooting for later, so I put the rifle down on the deckhouse as I cleared it, heading for the bow and the four new men. I went in swinging and had the advantage of a good start. My first blow was a wild one that caught a man coming in. He grunted, and then I was right in the middle of the wildest fist-swinging brawl I'd found in a coon's age.

Only I had the advantage again. There were four of them, and they had to hunt a target and be careful not to hit each other. All I had to do was punch. I rolled my shoulders up near my chin and went in with short arm punches. Then, when somebody grabbed at my head, I took him by both legs and dumped him over my head.

I backhanded another with a blow that probably jarred his relatives wherever they were. Somebody clobbered me on the side of the head. I got my back into the V of the bow, and they closed in on me. I ducked a punch, hitting hard with my right into his belly. He gasped like he'd been hit with a bath of cold water, and I swung him across in front of me and struck past his head at an open face. An open face that now had fewer teeth. A body splashed in the water, and then another. After the fourth splash, I saw LeBrun with a hatchet, chopping at the line.

The hatchet cut through, and the keelboat slipped away. The tide was in. Somebody fired a musket from the steamboat.

"The hell with that!" It was Macklem shouting. "Sink 'em!"

And they had the cannon to do it.

"Get the sail up, damn it!" I yelled.

We saw the flash of the gun and heard its boom. We heard a shot splash aft of us. Then another flash, which hit a bulwark and threw splinters in every direction. Some small ones stung my face. Down on one knee behind the bulwark, I aimed a little higher than where the flash had come from and squeezed off my shot.

Somebody yelled, but the musket flared again. He must have had the match in his hand. Another shot struck us, but struck at an angle and glanced off into the night.

Suddenly, the steamer's engines began to pound, and her wheel threshed.

"If she gets loose," it was McQuarrie beside me, "we're through. Macklem's got some crack gunners aboard there."

We stood in silence, staring off in the dark. We all knew what it meant. With steam they were faster, they could outmaneuver us, and we'd be dead . . . all of us.

"We've got to go ashore," I said. "We've got to leave the keelboat."

"What's that?" LeBrun had come forward, leaving Yvette at the rudder. "Leave my boat?"

"We have no choice. They'll shell it to bits. We can strike out overland."

"His men will track us down," LeBrun objected. "We'd have small chance."

"And no chance if we stay aboard," I said.

He looked at me angrily. But it was not at me his anger was directed. It was the nature of things. He knew it had to be done.

"There's a creek," he said. "It's shallow but partly hidden by an island . . ."

There was still an hour before dawn when we abandoned the keelboat.

CHAPTER 21

My black pants were shot, so I borrowed a pair from LeBrun, and a pair of elkhide moccasins. We took from the boat what we could.

We made a rowdy lot. Otis Pinkney became our leader. We followed—LeBrun and Yvette, then Mc-Quarrie, Jambe-de-Bois, and myself.

Pinkney led the way up a bank through some cottonwoods and out across a small meadow. That he had a destination in mind was obvious. He traveled fast, rarely looking back.

When we had traveled for an hour, he paused in a grove of huge old cottonwoods on a small branch of the creek that ran down toward the Missouri. There were a few wild plums, which we all ate, and we drank from the stream. He led off again after only a few minutes, but at a somewhat slower pace, keeping the trees between us and the river.

144

We were headed for Bonhomme Island.

For three days we traveled steadily. Several times we saw buffalo, and on the second day I killed a cow and we divided the meat, after eating what we could. We all made fresh moccasins from the hide. The green hide would not last as long as seasoned hide, but all of us had worn out our foot gear.

"We're near," Pinkney said on the fourth day. "From now on we take it easy. This here will be our last hot meal."

Earlier that day, we had killed a buffalo calf, and now we broiled steaks and ate well. Otis and LeBrun ate the liver, heart, and lights, and split the bones for the marrow. There were a few berries still on the bushes, but the birds had most of them, and there were signs that a bear had been feasting on them also.

All of us were on edge. We figured to meet the steamboat at the camp on Bonhomme Island. Now that we were close, none of us had a very good idea of what we should do. If there were as many men as we'd heard, we would have no chance at capturing the fort.

"The thing to do first," I said at last, "is capture the serpent."

"Supposing your Miss Majoribanks isn't aboard?" LeBrun suggested.

The same thought worried me. I told them so. "We'll have to chance it," I said. "We'll have to move in fast and quietly, take the boat, and then if Tabi . . . if Miss Majoribanks has been put ashore, we'll have to find her." I didn't mention that I hoped she was still alive.

At dusk we moved out. Suddenly, Pinkney put a hand on my arm and pointed. Through the leaves and across the river, narrower here, we could see the fires, at least a dozen of them, with a few lodges scattered here and there. It was obvious enough from the size of the fires, this was a white man's camp, although Indians might be present.

I wiped my palms on my pants. My mouth felt suddenly dry. There might be between fifty and a hundred men down there; there might be more.

Then, against the sky, I could see the smoke that could only be rising from the steamboat.

We had reached our rendezvous at last. We had arrived at Bonhomme Island.

Along the shore there were willows. We moved in among them.

The great firebreather was there, her huge head looming above us, jaws open, eyes distended.

All of us could swim. Stepping into the water, I led the way. I swam to the side of the hull. Catching hold of the rail, I climbed aboard. All was quiet. Only aft could I hear the low murmur of voices. One by one the others climbed quietly aboard. Then I started aft.

Suddenly, through an open porthole, Tabitha's voice came clearly. I felt weak with relief. Pausing, I listened.

"Of course not. Captain Macklem, what you suggest is impossible, and what you plan absurd."

"Absurd, is it?" I could sense under the casualness, the irritation in his voice. "We know what we are doing, Tabitha, our plans are made and are going forward. Even as we talk, some of our men are encamped not only here, but also near Fort Atkinson and near St. Louis.

"Our men are in Natchez and in New Orleans. We are ready to move against Fort Armstrong when I give the word. We have planned carefully. Within the next forty-eight hours, certain officials in New Orleans, Natchez, and St. Louis will be killed . . . in one way or another.

"With resistance paralyzed and communications cut off, we shall be in complete control. Once that happens, additional forces will move to join us."

"Captain Macklem," Tabitha's tone was assured. "You still have time to bring this farce to a close, to end your plots without being tried for treason. You see, Captain, you have been so confident you were moving in secrecy that you've failed to realize how obvious you've become."

"Obvious?"

"Of course. My office has had reports from New Orleans for years that something was in the wind. We knew of Torville's connection with it two years ago. My father's correspondents kept him advised of your efforts to recruit men in Mexico as well as New Orleans, and a year ago my father informed the general commanding the western districts.

"When you reentered the country from Quebec and murdered that poor Captain Foulsham, Talon made sure his murder was reported to the authorities. He did not say as much, but I believe he was quite sure who the murderer was."

"Yes," Macklem admitted, "that was a mistake. I should have killed him at once."

"You tried, didn't you? You see, Captain, you really haven't fooled anyone . . . not for a minute. Had you put the whole show upon the stage of the biggest theater in New York or Paris, you could not have had a more knowing audience."

"You talk very well, Tabitha." He was trying to maintain his calm, but his desperation was breaking through. "However, even if what you say is true, I still have you, and I have Charles."

She was silent for a moment, during which time I marveled at her self-possession. "Do you, Captain? Do you have us? How many of those men out there will remain loyal when they realize what has happened?"

Under my feet I felt the deck tilt ever so lightly. The boat was adrift! Surely, Macklem would notice it!

"To be guilty of such a plot as this," Tabitha said, "a man must be both a great egotist and an optimist. He must believe himself more shrewd and intelligent than anyone else. My father would never have put money in such an operation as this, Captain. It has too many loopholes. You must need, very desperately, to believe in it."

I was watching them now.

"One need not be shrewd to outwit a pack of fools. And those who are not fools are asleep. This land lies ready for the taking."

She smiled. "Every crackpot adventurer in the Western Hemisphere has believed that."

"Within forty-eight hours, it will be mine," he said complacently. But I knew her talk was reaching him.

"No," she replied, "you are wrong. You cannot win."

He got to his feet. "You are very sure of yourself, Tabitha," he said gently. "All of which makes bringing you to your knees more pleasant." He turned toward the door, then glanced back. "Tabitha, do you know where Charles is now?"

She turned sharply toward him, and he laughed.

"Amusing how tender a woman can feel toward her brother. We've decided to use Charles as an example, especially for you. We—"

Suddenly, he felt the movement in the deck and lunged for the door. At the same instant, there was a yell of alarm from aft, then a shot, followed by the rush of feet and the sound of clashing arms.

As Macklem reached the cabin door, I stepped into it.

He reacted instantaneously and struck out hard. I took the punch coming in. It struck with numbing force, but I'd driven hard, and we both staggered back into the cabin.

His left fist caught me over the eye with a blow like a club, and he threw a high right that I instinctively ducked, hitting him under the heart. Piling in close, I smashed away with both fists at his body, but was shoved off and hit again over my eye. I felt a trickle of blood from a cut, slipped inside his next punch, and slammed home two more.

His body was like iron, and he neatly turned aside, throwing me off balance. Before I could turn, he hit me just below the ear, but I took the punch standing and turned on him. I think he was shocked. He had expected me to fall. Instead, I looked at him and laughed.

I was hurt. I was badly shaken—had he known how badly, he could have killed me. We came together then, punching with both hands, and every blow he struck shook me to my heels.

He jerked his knee toward my crotch, but I brought a knee up across my other leg to block it. He shook me with a right to the head and stepped in, his fingers clawing for my eyes. I sank my face against his shoulder and ripped short, brutal punches to his gut.

He shoved me off, and for an instant we faced each other.

"You can fight," he said contemptuously, breathing hard. "You can fight just a little. Now I am going to kill you!"

He came in fast, and I threw a righthand punch at his face. He went under it and grabbed my left leg, lifting it high as he jammed his palm against my face. As he did so, he slid his leg behind mine, and I went over it backward to the floor. He followed in immediately, but he had not figured on my coming up fast. I had hit the deck hard, but hit it rolling, and was quickly on my feet moving into him.

He slipped on the rolling deck, and I caught his left arm in a hammerlock, pushing it toward his shoulder. He turned, throwing his right across my two arms, locking them behind his back. Then he threw me over his leg to the deck.

This time I was slower getting up, and he caught me in the wind with a vicious kick. I felt a stab of pain and gasped for breath, on my knees. He tried to step back to get distance, but I threw myself forward, grabbing his legs.

They were like iron, and he stood over me, laughing. Then he smashed his knee against the side of my face and knocked me sprawling under a table. He kicked me twice before I could get out, the second kick on the side of the neck and shoulder as I was coming up.

My right caught him on the chin, a short, wicked hook from close in, and it shook him. He stepped off, measured me with a left, missed a right as I came in close, and he tried to rabbit-punch me behind the neck. Strong as he was, I began to realize I was stronger still, and I bulled him back against the bulkhead, where I hit him twice in the body.

Suddenly, there was a terrible concussion from above as a gun was fired, then a second and a third. From Bonhomme Island there were wild yells . . . another shot.

My face was bloody. There was blood running into my eyes. His own face was smooth and hard as iron, unblemished. Yet, I could see there was no longer the same supreme self-confidence. I had him fighting for his life . . . as I was.

He sparred a moment. He jabbed at my face, and I went under it. He had half stepped back and was waiting with his right cocked for me to come in. Instead, I feinted, then smashed him on the chin with a right. His eyes blinked, and I hit him again.

Now he circled warily. For the first time, I think, he fully realized he might not win. In the narrow confines of the cabin, we moved toward each other.

Tabitha, who had drawn back into a corner, was watching wide eyed. My pistols lay near her, where they had slipped from my belt as I'd gone to the floor.

There was the pound of rushing feet on the deck outside. A cannon roared again. By the feel of the boat, we were now well into the current. Suddenly, Macklem half crouched, his hand went to his boot and came up with a knife. "Sorry!" he said. "But I've business aloft!"

He lunged with the blade, not slashing as he should have, but using his knife like a sword.

Slapping his knife hand with my left to push it

away from my body, I grabbed his wrist with my right and, stepping across in front of him, punched him to the deck. Yet a sudden lurch of the vessel threw me, and I fell along side and facing him.

My two pistols were there. He grabbed for one, I for the other. We both fired.

I felt a sudden burn as from a red-hot iron across my shoulder, and he was staring at me, his mouth open and his lower jaw gone. I fired again, and he slumped on the deck. I got slowly to my feet and fell back against the bulkhead.

Somebody loomed in the doorway, and I turned, half blind with blood and sweat.

"Don't shoot!" It was Jambe-de-Bois. "It's all right. It's all over."

I was gasping for breath as though I'd never get enough in my lungs. I tilted my head back against the bulkhead.

McQuarrie came over and began to wipe the blood from my face. "We found Charlie. Butlin got him loose and brought him to us. Then we opened fire on their camp. We shot into their campfire. It scattered them."

"Is anybody hurt?"

"A few scratches. We've been very lucky."

"Macklem is dead," Macaire was saying, and there was a lot of confused talk. LeBrun and Yvette were safe. So were Mrs. Higgs and Edwin Hale.

Tabitha was standing where she'd stood during the fight. She was still staring at me, only now she was trembling.

"You'd better sit down," I suggested, and she crossed over and sat down beside me.

"Macklem was Torville?" I asked, and she nodded.

"Where to?" asked Jambe-de-Bois.

"Pittsburgh," I said. "I've got a boat to build." I looked around at Tabitha. "Want to come along?"

"Yes," she said, "I've never built a boat."

ABOUT THE AUTHOR

LOUIS L'AMOUR, born Louis Dearborn L'Amour of French-Irish stock, is a descendant of François René, Vicompte de Chateaubriand, noted French writer, statesman, and epicure. Although Mr. L'Amour claims his writing began as a "spur-of-the-moment thing," prompted by friends who relished his verbal tales of the West, he comes by his talent honestly. A frontiersman by heritage (his grandfather was scalped by the Sioux), and a universal man by experience, Louis L'Amour lives the life of his fictional heroes. Since leaving his native Jamestown, North Dakota, at the age of fifteen, he's been a longshoreman, lumberjack, elephant handler, hay shocker, flume builder, fruit picker, and an officer on tank destroyers during World War II. And he's written four hundred short stories and over fifty books (including a volume of poetry).

Mr. L'Amour has lectured widely, traveled the West thoroughly, studied archaeology, compiled biographies of over one thousand Western gunfighters, and read prodigiously (his library holds more than two thousand volumes). And he's watched thirty-one of his westerns as movies. He's circled the world on a freighter, mined in the West, sailed a dhow on the Red Sea, been shipwrecked in the West Indies, stranded in the Mojave Desert. He's won fifty-one of fifty-nine fights as a professional boxer and pinch-hit for Dorothy Kilgallen when she was on vacation from her column. Since 1816, thirty-three members of his family have been writers. And, he says, "I could sit in the middle of Sunset Boulevard and write with my typewriter on my knees; temperamental I am not."

Mr. L'Amour is re-creating an 1865 Western town, christened Shalako, where the borders of Utah, Arizona, New Mexico, and Colorado meet. Historically authentic from whistle to well, it will be a live, operating town, as well as a movie location and tourist attraction.

Mr. L'Amour now lives in Los Angeles with his wife Kathy, who helps with the enormous amount of research he does for his books. Soon, Mr. L'Amour hopes, the children (Beau and Angelique) will be helping too.

LANDO by LOUIS L'AMOUR

Lando Sackett got to Texas with a well oiled hogleg, a racing mule that didn't look worth its salt, and a damn good idea of the whereabouts of buried gold across the border in Mexico.

In Mexico he had bad luck. His party had to run for it, and when Lando stood rearguard they pulled out and left him.

Six years in a Mexican prison put muscles in his arms, fire in his heart, and pure recklessness in his head.

When he caught up with the men who betrayed him it didn't matter that he had no gun – he fought alone and barefisted!

0 552 09354 8 – 65p

THE SACKETT BRAND by LOUIS L'AMOUR

There's a Sackett in trouble. Forty gunslingers from the Lazy A had got Tell Sackett cornered back under the Mogollon Rim. They'd fixed to hang him if they could get him alive, fill him extra full of lead if they couldn't.

But the Sacketts, they don't cotton to that kind of treatment. Hunt one Sackett and you hunt 'em all. They came from all over – mountain Sacketts, flat-land Sacketts, politicians, outlaws, cattle-men, bankers, tinkers – and all of them rarin' to fight.

0 552 08678 9 – 65p

TO THE FAR BLUE MOUNTAINS by LOUIS L'AMOUR

From some men, an acre of land and a cottage are enough; not for Barnabas Sackett – the wanderlust in his blood drove him from the peaceful fen country of England over the sea to the New World. The call of the West was strong, and with Abigail beside him – and a Queen's warrant for his arrest behind him – Barnabas turned his face to the far blue mountains of Virginia ... He and his followers fought off wild beasts, shot buffalo and just about kept themselves alive – and at last they built their stockade on the James River. For a while, all was peaceful. Then one night, there were noises outside the stockade and, in a flare of torch-light, a dozen savage, painted faces ...

0 522 10550 3 – 65p

WESTWARD THE TIDE by LOUIS L'AMOUR

The wagon trains were pushing further and further West, carrying men in search of adventure, or in search of gold from the Black Hills. Matt Bardoul had craved – and won – both in his time, but now he needed more: one look at old man Coyle's daughter and he knew why he'd agreed to join the trek. Yet there was the lure of gold too – a fortune for the taking up in the Big Horns, where the Sioux still roamed ... There would be trouble on the trail too, with Gunmen like Logan Deane along and the gold-lust in every man's mind. Matt figured there'd be a heavier price paid for that Big Horn Gold ...

0 552 10483 3 – 60p

SHANE by JACK SCHAEFER

'CALL ME SHANE.' He rode into our valley in the summer of '89 a slim man dressed in black, riding easily. He never told us more than his name.

'There's something about him,' Mother said, 'something . . . dangerous.'

'He's dangerous all right,' Father replied, 'but not us.'

'He's like a slow-burning fuse,' the mule skinner said. 'So quiet, you forget it's burning till it sets off trouble. And there's trouble brewing . . . '
There was.

One of the greatest novels ever to come out of the American West.

0 552 10968 1 – 65p

SUDDEN – THE MARSHAL OF LAWLESS by OLIVER STRANGE

'Being Marshal of Lawless is plain suicide!' That's what they told the young fellow who applied for the job. They figured that anyone who had hocked his horse, his saddle and his guns to get money for liquor, was not the kind of man who could hold down one of the toughest towns in the West.

But then the young stranger redeemed his guns and strapped them on. Lawless looked again. 'Gentlemen, hush!' said one inhabitant. 'A man has come to town!'

0 552 08906 0 – 60p

A SELECTED LIST OF CORGI WESTERNS FOR YOUR READING PLEASURE

WHILE EVERY EFFORT IS MADE TO KEEP PRICES LOW, IT IS SOMETIMES NECESSARY TO INCREASE PRICES AT SHORT NOTICE. CORGI BOOKS RESERVE THE RIGHT TO SHOW AND CHARGE NEW RETAIL PRICES ON COVERS WHICH MAY DIFFER FROM THOSE ADVERTISED IN THE TEXT OR ELSEWHERE.

THE PRICES SHOWN BELOW WERE CORRECT AT THE TIME OF GOING TO PRESS (MARCH '79).

J. T. EDSON

☐ 10332 2	OLE DEVIL AND THE MULE TRAIN No. 79		50p
☐ 10406 X	DOC LEROY, M.D. No. 80		50p
☐ 10505 8	OLE DEVIL AT SAN JACINTO No. 81		60p
☐ 10660 7	SET A-FOOT No. 82		65p
☐ 10769 7	BEGUINAGE No. 83		65p
☐ 10880 4	BEGUINAGE IS DEAD No. 84		65p

LOUIS L'AMOUR

☐ 10853 7	THE MOUNTAIN VALLEY WAR		65p
☐ 10550 3	TO THE FAR BLUE MOUNTAINS		65p
☐ 10483 3	WESTWARD THE TIDE		60p

OLIVER STRANGE

☐ 08810 2	SUDDEN – OUTLAWED		60p
☐ 08728 9	SUDDEN PLAYS A HAND		60p
☐ 08811 0	SUDDEN		60p

JOHN J. McLAGLEN

☐ 10720 4	HERNE THE HUNTER 7: DEATH RITES		60p
☐ 10788 3	HERNE THE HUNTER 8: CROSS-DRAW		60p
☐ 10834 0	HERNE THE HUNTER 9: MASSACRE!		65p

All these books are available at your bookshop or newsagent; or can be ordered direct from the publisher. Just tick the titles you want and fill in the form below.

CORGI BOOKS, Cash Sales Department, P.O. Box 11, Falmouth, Cornwall.

Please send cheque or postal order, no currency.

U.K. send 22p for first book plus 10p per copy for each additional book ordered to a maximum charge of 82p to cover the cost of postage and packing.

B.F.P.O. and Eire allow 22p for first book plus 10p per copy for the next 6 books, thereafter 4p per book.

Overseas customers please allow 30p for the first book and 10p per copy for each additional book.

NAME (block letters)..

ADDRESS ....

(MARCH 1979) ....